SEASIDE JOURNEYS
OF FAITH

Written and Illustrated by

Jay Diedreck

ISBN 978-1-64492-588-1 (paperback)
ISBN 978-1-64492-589-8 (digital)

Christian Faith Publishing, Inc.
832 Park Avenue
Meadville, PA 16335
www.christianfaithpublishing.com

Printed in the United States of America

To my precious wife, Alicia

Dear reader,

This book is a work of fiction. All the people and events portrayed on these pages are fictitious. Some of the places in this story are also fictitious. Other than those locations, any similarity to reality is totally coincidental.

Jay Diedreck

CONTENTS

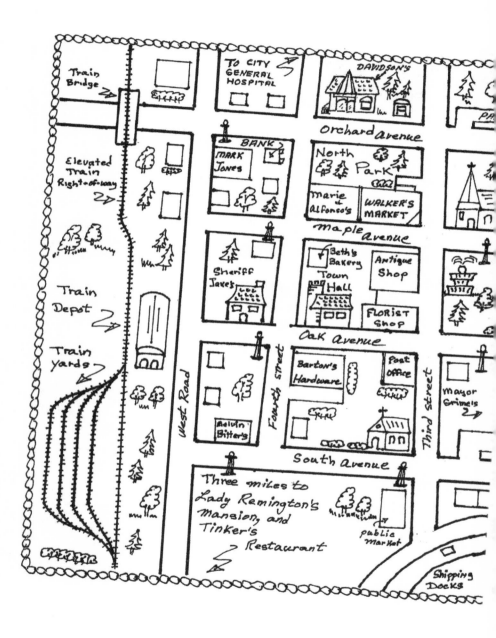

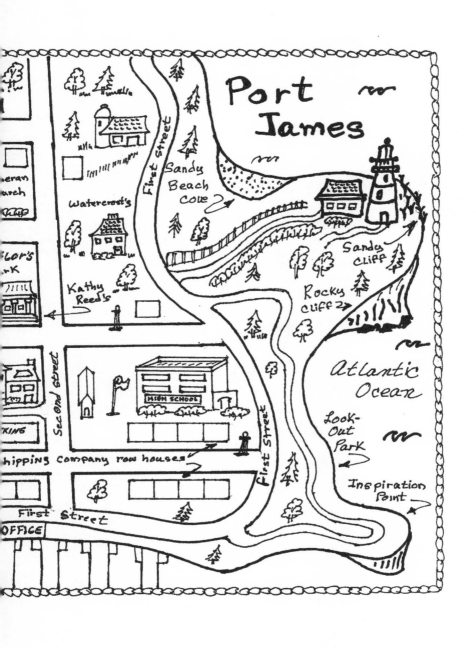

A Bit of Family History

In an early morning of 1880, the fog had not yet lifted from resting on the water. The captain of an English ocean steamer sent his order from the bridge; slowing its engines to quarter speed. Just appearing through the captain's sea-sprayed windows was the impressive skyline of New York City and New York Harbor. After twelve days at sea, it was a welcome sight to the sailors and equally for the rows and rows of immigrants.

From his advantage point, the captain viewed the passengers crowding to the leeward side of his vessel for their first look. It was a weary trip, but this was the first sign of their new and exciting life. Not on this trip with this vessel, but within seven more years in October 28, 1886, the Statue of Liberty would also greet arrivals.

One couple remained underdeck, the husband holding his wife's hand. Lying flat on the bare wooden deck boards, she was experiencing hard contractions fifteen minutes apart. Nataly Walker, a woman of eighteen young years, said nothing, but her innocent and beautiful brown eyes expressed her frightened state to her husband, Joshua.

Sometimes, sanitary conditions on board were less than adequate. In fact, on this same vessel, a few souls looking for a better life succumbed to their deaths. Lacking fresh air on the sleeping deck, a sneeze and cough had spread throughout the passengers. It could have infected all sixty-seven on board had most passengers not kept a cotton hanky around their nose and mouth. From previous passages, the deckhands always knew to keep their distance from the passengers.

So it was among these conditions that their first baby was preparing to be born. With a quiet prayer to his God, Joshua pleaded mercifully for another hour of delay. Opening his eyes from prayer, Joshua heard and felt the reverse thrusts of the ship's engines. The vessel slowed, finding its proper place along the New York City Pier.

Deckhands above them guided the immigrants from the steamer's main deck to the gangplank leading to the city pier. Frightened and alone, the Walkers remained below, inside the lower deck. After a few minutes, a crewman opened the door to where they huddled together. A cascade of sunlight flooded onto the couple. Outside, the fog had lifted, and the warmth of the July summer took its place. With compassion in his eyes, the crewman looked at them both, then kneeled down next to Nataly.

"Madam, do you speak English?" he asked.

They both nodded yes. Offering his hand, and with Joshua's help, they managed to carefully get Nataly to her feet. With God's help, the three slowly struggled down the gangway toward City Pier. When their feet finally touched the wooden dock, the crewman wished them well, then left so he could finish his duties on the ocean steamer.

Joshua and Nataly followed the crowd through American customs. Once custom officers saw their predicament, the Walkers were quickly brought to the side to complete paperwork. Within minutes, they found themselves in the bustle of New York City. Looking up and down the city avenue, Joshua finally saw their friends Joan and Luke Miles crossing on the other side to greet them. It did not take long for the Miles to understand that Nataly was ready to give birth to a new life in this world.

Joan ran up to her dear friends. With great concern in her voice, she looked directly into Nataly's eyes and said, "Darling, Luke and I will walk you to the nearest city clinic. They can take care of you there. I believe they never close their doors."

SEASIDE JOURNEYS OF FAITH

Luke and Joshua crisscrossed their hands with each other, making a human chair for Nataly to sit on their arms. Among the street noise and bustle of horse-drawn carts and carriages, they scurried down the city sidewalk, Nataly's arms around both of the men's shoulders. With Joan hurrying ahead of them in the lead, they reached the clinic's door with almost no time left. As soon as they opened the clinic's doors and entered the lobby, the staff saw the group of four and immediately placed dear Nataly on a stretcher with wheels, with Joshua walking along the side of his young wife.

Another staff person opened the room where a midwife, named Iris, was waiting. She held a white sheet, which was folded under her arm. To her right was a cart with a drawer that had a few medical tools that were available if needed. Extending a soothing, reassuring smile and with soft dulcimer tones, she greeted Nataly.

"Honey, everything will be all right. Is this your first baby? Let's take a look and see how you are progressing."

Iris looked at Joshua and motioned him to leave the room. He was to stay in the waiting room just down the hall.

Nataly instantly started to cry uncontrollably. "I want my husband here! I want my husband here...right next to me! Don't take my husband away from me!"

Even though Iris never had a father stay in the room before, understanding completely, she assured Nataly that he could remain. Looking at Joshua, Iris whispered to him kindly, but in a way, he understood completely.

"Just reassure her and be calm. Hold her hand...no matter how hard she may squeeze it. Understand? Besides being her loving husband, you will also have to be her rock."

Joshua nodded yes and took his place on his young wife's side while reaching for her hand. Iris felt Nataly's abdomen tenderly yet firmly. She had trained hands from many years of midwifery practice. Iris paused for a moment then said:

"Nataly, your baby's head is crowning.
When I say so, please push. Hold on, darling...
now push. Great, now rest a few seconds. I will

11

tell you when to push again. Take some deep breaths for me now."

Iris sensed that there was something going wrong with this delivery, but she knew she shouldn't show any concern to the mom. The baby's umbilical cord was wedged between its left shoulder and Nataly's birth canal. Very soon, the little one would literally be without the life support from the cord, including oxygen. Iris knew it would be only a few minutes, and she would be delivering a stillbirth instead of a healthy baby.

She whispered to Joshua, "If you are a praying man, please say a prayer for your wife, your baby, and a prayer for me. I will need our good Lord Jesus's help right now."

Nataly sensed Iris's concern and started to cry again. She squeezed her husband's hand, partly due to the pain as well as for comfort. Joshua closed his eyes and said a prayer for God's immediate help. He then prayed for forgiveness because of taking his dear wife to America so close to her time of her giving birth. Joshua opened his eyes from his quick prayer and thought about their new but uncertain place where they would have to make a living for themselves. Joshua held back his tears as he thought of the peril he made for his young eighteen-year-old wife.

Iris maneuvered her fingertips, reaching for the umbilical cord, trying to ease it into the proper position. With the direction from God above, her fingers found the cord. She maneuvered it around the baby's shoulders, then quickly reached for the forceps. She gently pulled the baby a little. Looking at Nataly, she said firmly:

"Honey, it's time to push! Give it all you got, my dear. You have a baby to bring into this world!"

With all the strength she could muster, Nataly delivered her pelvic push, then after a few moments, experienced the most heavenly sound a mother could hear—the little breath and the cry of her firstborn baby.

Without the slightest knowledge of how close he came to death, Samuel Walker was born on July 18, 1880. Now they were a family of three.

§

Two days later, in the morning, Joan and Luke came back again to the clinic. They were greeted by the clinic's receptionist and were told that Nataly and Joshua were now able to leave. After a few minutes, the new parents with their healthy baby boy appeared in the doorway. Joan rushed up to Nataly, hugging her gently and said:

"Oh honey, you have been through a lot. How do you feel? Know that you are welcomed to stay with us as long as you want."

Nataly said, "I'm doing pretty well. They took good care of me here. We are so grateful to have good friends like you two. Thank you so much! Oh, I think I see Iris coming in to say goodbye."

Even though Nataly knew Iris for only two days, she gave her a hug and a kiss on the right cheek.

"Thank you, Iris. You were the best, and thank you for letting Joshua stay with me! I hope you don't mind me saying that I am so happy you are a Christian woman…especially because of your vocation. God bless you and your work!"

The four of them, along with the newborn Samuel Walker wrapped in his white blanket, his nose and little eyes peeking out, found their way to the corner to wait for the horse-drawn street trolley. In a few minutes, they were seated and on their way to Miles's new three-story brownstone in the New York City borough of Queens.

§

Thirty years before Joshua and Nataly's arrival to America, the sewing machine was invented. It was one of many machines that was born during the Industrial Revolution of the late 1790s to the mid-1800s. Vast numbers of immigrants from Germany, Poland, Russia, and Italy, who were desperately willing enough, ended up working in America's large, dirty, and polluted cities. Many immigrants worked ten-hour days in textile sweatshops, making clothing for the lower and middle class. The steel and coal industry also needed hundreds to work long hours and perform many dangerous duties. No matter in what kind of industry people worked, conditions were far from pleasant. Without adequate workplace standards, many died on the job with no financial benefits to bring home to the rest of the family.

While living in England, Joshua and Nataly had both inherited enough money from their parents to afford the trip to America with some extra money to spare. They made a promise to themselves, which was not to work in the sweatshops of New York City or the coal mines of Pennsylvania.

The Miles were wonderful friends and hosted them graciously for as long as the Walkers wanted. After a little over one week, they got back their land legs from the long ocean trip, and Nataly recovered her strength from giving birth. On the steps of their brownstone home, the Walkers bided their friends farewell and headed to coastal Maine with their new baby boy. Luckily for newborn Samuel, once his parents got to the coast, they decided to make Port James, Maine, their forever home.

Over the years, growing up in Port James, Samuel became a fine young man that took the eyes of many ladies. At the age of twenty, in the year of our Lord 1900, one Saturday morning, Samuel met Beatrice Brown at the public market in town, located at Sailor's Park on Second Street and Oak Avenue. They fell in love and were married after only five dates.

In the spring of 1911, within their own home, at the age of thirty-one, Beatrice gave birth to a healthy baby boy, whom they named Adam.

Like so many families in this era, immediate gratification was not even thought of. If something was worth buying, it was worth waiting for until money was saved. Such it was with Samuel and Beatrice. In 1917, with much scrimping and saving, at the age of thirty-seven years old, they were able to open a corner grocery store in Port James. Although the mainstay of the store was fresh fruits and vegetables, they stocked a variety of canned goods and even some handy household items. Beatrice always made sure the market also had a nice display of home-baked pies, cookies, and breads. The little market was appropriately and simply named Walker's. Their son, Adam, was six years old when the Walker's had their market's grand opening.

JAY DIEDRECK

Birth Date and Birthplace of the Walker Men

1860 Joshua Walker born in England. Wife is Nataly.
1880 Samuel Walker born in N.Y.C. clinic. Wife is Beatrice.
1911 Adam Walker born in Port James. Wife is Silvia.
1935 Walt Walker born in Port James.

CHAPTER

2

Courtship of 1935

With the busyness of life, time melted away like an ice cream cone in a toddler's hand on a hot August day. Even though it was hard for Samuel and Beatrice to believe, they had owned and operated Walker's Market for eighteen years. Their son, Adam, was now twenty-five years old and certainly reaching manhood. His parents celebrated each and every one of his birthdays but had not thought much about his desire to meet and date women. Even though dating was a normal part of entering manhood, Adam had little time for such things. He had helped out at the market since he was eight and now, even at the age of twenty-five, had not even gone on his first date.

Adam, like most boys, played his share of high school sports but always had an eye for gorgeous Silvia. She was not in many of his classes since she had elected to take business classes while Adam took the normal course of instruction. As Adam's luck would have it, Silvia and her family kept Port James as their only place to live. They loved this little Maine village, within its gas-lit Victorian streets and avenues, its residents—just about everything about it. In fact, at the age of thirty years, Silvia's parents even bought two cemetery plots in West Side Cemetery, just a short drive south.

Silvia was a lovely and strong-headed young lady, especially for her age. After high school, she worked in Barton's Hardware store, located on Oak Avenue and Fourth Street, helping with their accounts. She was very accurate in balancing their business ledgers of the store's income and expenditures.

Samuel and Beatrice should have found it a little peculiar that their son was all too eager to go to Barton's Hardware to get whatever the market might need. It didn't matter if it was a new straw broom or another bag of wood shavings. The wood shavings were thrown onto the floor when cleaning. This kept the dust down while pushing a broom and absorbed any water or oils that a customer could accidently slip on. After sweeping, the wood shavings were collected in a dustpan and thrown away with the dirt.

Samuel eyed his son as he picked up the corn broom for the third time in one day and started to spread the shavings on the floor. Samuel noticed his son even swept the floor when there were customers around. That was really not appropriate.

"Beatrice," Samuel said to his wife. "Why... I think our Adam has a screw missing in his head. This is the third time today that he picked up that broom. I have also noticed that even though the wood shaving bag is still more than half full, he starts on me about buying some more. The last few times, he bought the five-pound bag at Barton's instead of the forty-pound bag. He came back three quarters of an hour later with the bag and a great, big Hollywood smile on his face. I believe all this has got to do with that lovely girl who helps out at Barton's Hardware."

Beatrice looked at Samuel and replied, "You think?"

"Yes, honey, and I want to approach Adam about this girl, but I don't want to embarrass the boy. I have to think about this. Don't worry. I will judge my words just right...let me think it all over."

By that time, Adam had finished his sweeping task and was thinking of asking his dad for some pocket change to go to Barton's for window glass cleaner. While standing near the front of the market, Samuel pondered what was going on around him. Meanwhile, way in the back, Adam was hanging up the broom, putting it away for the third time.

At about this moment, there were twelve customers mulling around, trying to decide what food they might want to buy for dinner. In the presence of everyone in the store, Samuel cupped his hands around his mouth like a megaphone and yelled to Adam:

"Hey, son, do you like that girl, Silvia, who
works at *Barton's*? Your mom and I think you do,
so for crying out loud in a bucket, ask her out on
a date sometime soon!"

The market became as quiet as midnight on a country farm.
Then a few customers started to laugh, which followed a grand
applause that lasted until Adam ran out the front door on his mission.

Adam reached Barton's in record time. Standing outside the
entrance, his legs felt weak, not from the two-minute run, but from
his nervousness and anxiety. He had never asked a girl out, and so he
decided to practice by talking to the gas streetlamp pole between the
road and the sidewalk. Looking directly at the lamp pole, but imag-
ining Silvia's face, he said:

"Uh, Silvia, would you put up with me long
enough to go on a date with you? No, that's not
too good. Let me start again. Would you be willing... I mean...would you like to go on a date
with me, maybe at the cinema for a movie or
maybe a picnic at Gray Cliff lighthouse?"

"Why, Mr. Walker!"
Silvia's voice came from behind him, and in a flash, Adam
turned on his heels, stumbled once, and found himself face-to-face
with the gorgeous Silvia. She looked as captivating as the colored
painting of the mermaid he had taped above his bed at home.

"Mr. Walker, were you talking to me?"
Adam was intelligent enough but, on the spur of the moment,
did not think very fast.

"Oh no, uh, Silvia... I was talking to the streetlamp."
Silvia assessed his innocent facial expression and replied:

"Too bad, Adam, because I would have
gone out with you...but for future reference, I
don't think you are getting anywhere with that

streetlamp. Besides, I think she is a bit too tall for you."

With that interaction, Silvia turned around and headed home. Her hips moved rhythmically and innocently seductive as she walked down the sidewalk. Adam thought he botched the whole thing until he saw her wiggle a little approving wave with the tips of her fingers. That little wave…it surged his whole being with male hormones that he never experienced before. He was in love. Looking towards the sky, he said:

"Thank you, God, for making such a beautiful woman as Silvia. I love her sparking deep-blue eyes and her shiny black hair, not to mention her freckles. I truly hope to see her again, Lord, but even if not, thanks anyway. She is a perfect creation! Oh! I almost forgot. Amen."

From that encounter on, and for the next few weeks, Silvia made sure that she and Adam had "chance" meetings. She knew when he would take his walks and of course, she just happen to join him. It was a few months and several official dates later when Silvia invited Adam out for a picnic at Gray Cliff light.

Before leaving home, Silvia had packed a lunch, which she placed in a brown wicker picnic basket. She included roast beef sandwiches, lemonade, and two turnovers from Beth's Bakery. Silvia placed napkins and a red and white tablecloth on the top. Before closing the wicker lid, she gave one more glance. Taking inventory of items in her picnic basket, she said to herself:

> "Well, I think that is everything. I hope Adam is on time. He truly is a special man, not to mention his good looks. Okay, everything is all set."

Adam left the market in enough time to meet the gorgeous Silvia at her home promptly at noon, the time *she* decided. When Adam walked around the corner of her block, he could see Silvia at her home, a short ways away. Silvia was waiting on her front steps, with the picnic basket next to her on the concrete.

Adam said to himself, "Gosh, she is simply beautiful, and look at that strawhat she is wearing. I love it!"

As if on cue, Silvia tipped her hat on her head, giving it an awesomely darling and stylish appearance to her attire.

Her top, a white cotton short-sleeve blouse was buttoned in the front and up to her neck. Adam loved Silvia's spray of freckles on the top side of her arms, and when he was close enough, the cluster of freckles on and around her nose seemed to delightfully tease him. He noticed at these times that his heart was beating faster as well as his breathing.

As soon as Silvia saw Adam, she jumped on her tiptoes and sent him a wave and a smile. He felt he could not walk fast enough to get up to where she was waiting. Holding out her hands, Silvia blessed him with a warm hug and a sweet kiss on his cheek.

"Let's get going, Adam. The day is simply beautiful! Oh… thanks for being on time."

She bent down and picked up her picnic basket and gave it to Adam for him to carry. It was only a few minutes to the lighthouse. While walking, she touched Adam's fingers, which then progressed to holding hands. As they walked, Adam became more and more in love. Feeling her tender hand in his, he could have strolled with her for hours, but just past the village streets, the top of the lighthouse was already in view. A left turn took them onto a sandy footpath.

Once near the light, Silvia found a flat spot on the grass, then took the picnic basket from Adam to set up lunch. While on her knees, she smoothed the red-and-white-checkered cloth on the ground, then looked up at Adam as she took the food and plates out for them. "Adam dearest, you know that this is our ten-week anniversary?"

Adam wondered if this time event in their courtship required a presentation of flowers or something similar. Well, he thought, there should be a book about this sort of event. Men just don't keep track of these things like the women folk of this society. Silvia reached out and held Adam's hand and continued:

"You must also know that I have a suitable
level of affection for you."

Silvia always admired the women who left the house during the First World War and worked in factories that produced ammunition and many other war supplies. Fighting overseas, their husbands and brothers left a void in the workforce, so American housewives filled that need. Women were more than a symbol. In very positive ways, they demonstrated the usefulness and fortitude of women. They got the job done, helping both men and women in our armed forces. Without their important roles and the war products they manufactured, America would not have fared as well.

Silvia also loved to read about Susan B. Anthony, from Rochester, New York. She was born in 1820 and, even at an early age, wanted to change injustices in America that were just considered the norm. Susan gathered antislavery petitions at the age of seventeen, and at the age of forty-six, she became the New York state agent for the antislavery society. When Susan was fifty-two years old, she was arrested for voting in her hometown of Rochester. Delivering over seventy-five speeches, her spirited work finally led to the Nineteenth Amendment, giving women the right to vote in America.

So with all this flowing around her brain, Silvia felt she also was a progressive woman in her own right. She could and would present her feelings perfectly well and without reservations to her man friend—whether he was ready for it or not.

Silvia took a small bite from her sandwich and blotted her lips with her napkin. Placing it down on her lap, she looked directly at her boyfriend and said:

> "Adam, you also know that if we get married, your parents will expect us to eventually own and operate Walker's Market."

Up to this point in their courtship, ticklish topics like this had not entered their minds, at least not his. Adam put down his half-eaten roast beef sandwich onto his picnic plate. Wiping his mouth on his linen napkin, he knew not what to expect and became a little worried. With the new uncertainty between them, he decided to chew everything well and then carefully swallow. He certainly did not want to eat any food that he would suddenly inhale and go down the wrong pipe. Silvia waited a moment or two to let the message of marriage sink in and to also asses Adam's facial and body language. Then plowing right into it, as a progressive woman would, she continued sharing her expectations:

> "I think you know that I love our time together, and you are quite a dignified, good-looking gentleman that any levelheaded woman would love to share her life with. I place myself in that category…"

Adam was at his wit's end by this point. Meagerly, he tried his best to make sense of what she was stating. He was at a total lost when she said things like *levelheaded woman* and *category*. What was coming next? He decided to finish one last swig of lemonade before she continued:

> "Adam, don't look so worried! Way before I met you, I thought about this. Please just hear me out. I just merely wanted to know if you would adventure with me to the Belgian Congo on an elephant hunt."

Silvia couldn't keep her laughter restrained within her for more than a few seconds, but it was worth it. She watched poor Adam looking like a donkey just kicked him squarely in the back of his head. She could almost visualize question marks flying from his brain and piling up on the red-and-white-checkered tablecloth that she had laid down on the grass for their picnic.

"Oh, Adam, are you always going to be this easy to trick, or is it my natural, delicate beauty making you so stunned?"

Adam bought into her presentation that there were only two situations to pick from: her beauty or his boyish gullibility.

"Uh… I think it must be your beauty?"

"Adam, you are both a fast and extremely accurate thinker. That is why you deserve me. So anyway, I was just reminiscing about your parents. I have such admiration for them. It is as if I have known them for years. They are such special people. If I were them however…well, let me put it this way: I think they should have a life outside the market, and they should have always taken at least Sundays off…maybe even an occasional Monday. They deserve some vacations as well. What do you think? Adam, were you listening to me?"

Adam was scratching his right temple and wished his black-winged tipped dress shoes were not so tight.

"Silvia, I believe your thoughts have a certain amount of merit. As a youth growing up at the store, I have often thought about taking time away from work. Don't get me wrong—growing up with a family business was just fine… I mean, I did not know anything else. To have a whole Sunday off every week instead of just a few hours for church would have been a real blessing. A week vacation? How wonderful would that have been!"

Silvia noticed Adam did not address having an occasional Monday off from the store but decided not to push it. This request will come up again after they are married.

Just then, a flock of seagulls catching the ocean breeze flew overhead toward the lighthouse.

Minding the Business

The next few years included the marriage of Adam and Silvia in 1935. Silvia planned the wedding with three of her closest girlfriends. She was excited about both Adam and her writing their own wedding vows to each other. Silvia certainly gave her fiancé plenty of time to write his own vows to her, but he was quite busy. Nearly all his time was absorbed in keeping the market going with some help from his aging parents. Since he never sat down to write his wedding vow to her, Silvia wrote two very nice ones and gave Adam the chance to decide which one he wanted. In both vows that Adam was given to choose from, Silvia strategically included that they would promise some ample time for each other.

In 1936, nine months after their marriage in Our Lord's Lutheran Church, a baby boy was given to them from God. They name him Walt. He was baptized by pastor Westman in Our Lord's Lutheran Church when the infant boy was one month old. Now Adam, Silvia, and Walt became a young family of their own.

Even though Adam's parents, Samuel and Beatrice, were only fifty-five years old—like so many folks who worked so very hard— they were rapidly feeling their age. No matter how much pleasure they used to gain from things they did together in their past, every task now seemed too hard. With its long hours, Samuel and Beatrice worked with Adam and Silvia every day in the market. Eventually, the time had come that their parents would only drop in for a few hours each day. A full twelve-hour day on their feet, as well as lifting boxes, became too much for either of them.

So in 1936, the ownership of the market and the small apartment on the second floor was transferred completely over to Adam and Silvia. For better or for worse, this included not only all the profits but also all the management. Actually this made it easier for Adam and Silvia since any *day-to-day decisions* only had to be made by them. Their parents no longer had to be consulted. Luckily for the family, the business was in good hands.

Owning a market required mornings that started very early every day. No family member had time to linger in the bedrooms or bath. However, one morning while shaving, Adam looked in the mirror and saw a few more gray hairs growing around his temples. Except for this graying, he still had a thick head of curly black hair, but as he looked a little closer, he saw two or three tiny wrinkles appearing here and there on his face. At forty years old and feeling the march of time that waits for no one, Adam whispered into his mirror, "Is it really 1951 already?"

Adam and Silvia had owned the market for sixteen years now, and their son, Walt, was fifteen years old. To Adam, it didn't seem that long ago that in 1941, Silvia and he were thirty years old. Together with five-year-old Walt, they would gather around the Victrola radio in their apartment. The push-button tube radio and its console stood in the bay window. Tuning in the news station, they listened to President Roosevelt's radio updates concerning World War II. Adam remembered how his parents encouraged customers and friends to buy war bonds. Besides that, Silvia and Adam placed a poster in the market window stating such and another poster of "Rosie the Riveter." Rosie was depicted as a hardworking, muscular gal who left the house to work in factories during the war. Rosie was another woman hero of Silvia's.

For years, Adam had a philosophy that most humans are either generally good people, but if not, they are just misunderstood. Adam's mind sort of wandered into these and other thoughts when Walker's

Market was quiet of customers. Oh, of course, there were plenty of things to do in the market, and he would get to them all the same.

Silvia, working side by side with her husband, picked up any undone tasks that needed her attention; after all, it was their life and livelihood. They both felt blessed by their Creator to be part of Port James. Including their son, Walt, already four generations had lived in this quant Maine village. Surrounded by so many friends and a cluster of stores, homes, churches and gas-lit streets, several thousand souls called this place theirs—all perfectly perched on the rocky Atlantic coast near Gray Cliff lighthouse.

Other than greeting customers in the store and keeping the books, Silvia felt her task of rotating the market's fresh produce and canned goods was equally important. She made sure the oldest yet perfectly fine items were placed toward the front of the shelves. Neither Adam nor Silvia would ever sell stale bread or muffins, nor very old canned goods of any kind. Thankfully, most items sold fast enough that it almost never happened. If an apple had the slightest bruise or discoloration, out it would go into the bag for the dumpster next to the loading dock.

Silvia felt even more certain to keep the over-the-counter drugs fresh. They were located on two shelves just to the left of the cash register nearest the entrance. More often than needed, she kept in mind how long every item stayed on the shelves. There were no expiration dates to keep track of aging medicine, so Silvia kept all this on inventory receivable sheets. She would not sell things like aspirin, iodine, or mercurochrome older than one year. Port James villagers were her friends, and the same respect was given to the summer visitors.

From the very beginning, the market was called Walker's, and Adam and Silvia would never think of changing the name. Even from the outset, Samuel and Beatrice created a fine reputation within the village, and it grew through the years. Adam and Silvia continued this family's reputation by adding some more items here and there to sell besides the fresh produce and canned goods.

The entrance to Walker's was recessed into the building, giving shelter from the summer rain, having enough space for maybe five pedestrians or commuters. This serves as kind of a bus stop even though it never was an official bus shelter. The floor of this outside recessed area is surfaced in small black and white ceramic tile with the name Walker's spelled out as an inlay. From the floor and halfway up on either side is green-painted iron wainscoting. Above the wainscoting is plate glass windows which allows Adam and Silvia to show their fresh pies and produce through these windows.

A few years into ownership, Adam made a fruit stand out of wood. On pleasant weather days, he wheeled his blue-and-white-painted stand outside to display Maine blueberries, with apples, oranges, a single row of lemons, and bunches of bananas.

The Port James community is the salt of the earth and family-orientated. Her residents are hardworking. Many of the villager's livelihoods come from various ocean-related avenues. In this village, there are only a handful of well-to-do families.

The fact is on several occasions, a local customer would not have enough money to pay for everything right then and there. One day at the market, the sweet smell of a warm homemade blueberry pie triggered a little girl to pull on her mom's coat sleeve.

"Mom, can you just imagine how tasty that pie would be? I know we usually don't have dessert, but after all, it was my last day of second grade, and we should celebrate! Please, Mom, please? Pretty please, Mom?"

"Just be patient, Harriot. Let me count my change. I might have enough...especially for this occasion of ours."

Harriot's mom, Genny Tayler, looked into her hand-tooled leather pocketbook. The flap which folded over her pocketbook depicted a lighthouse, styled after the one of Port James, Gray Cliff lighthouse. She had eyed it in the lighthouse gift store when she and her husband were here on their honeymoon eleven years earlier. It was an extravagance at that time, but her new beau wanted to be her hero. Looking into the sparkle of his woman's green eyes, and without any more consideration on his behalf, he purchased it right on the spot. After their honeymoon, once a month, his new bride would rub saddle oil into the pocketbook's leather to keep it supple. The inside of her pocketbook had a light odor of leather, lipstick, and dollar bills, oddly enough not at all an unpleasant sensation.

Little Harriot sported a jet-black layered-cut hairdo, which ended with a short ponytail in the back. When she skipped down the sidewalk on her way to school, the cute little ponytail would swing left and right with each bounce. So now she was almost at the end of second grade, pleading for a little dessert. It didn't take any more intuition than a seven-year-old could possess to know there was no money. At least today, there would be no treat for her.

Just on the other side of the wooden counter, both Silvia and Adam were looking at the scenario unfolding before them. Silvia spoke first, but for both herself and hubby.

"Mrs. Tayler, may I make a suggestion? For special occasions as these, Adam and I would certainly extend to you a line of credit, if that would please you. We have several customers in Port James that don't always have enough cash on hand."

With that, Adam reached up toward the tin ceiling where a large wire hook held ten or more lunch-size brown paper bags. Each flat bag had a customer's name written on it, followed by a running total of what they owed. In turn, each customer kept track of their totals of both charges and their payments. There was no need for plastic credit cards with chips, passwords, or decrypted usernames. Yet in a wonderful and efficient way, it worked flawlessly and with compassion. One's good word and a hardy handshake started the line of credit, with no interest expected.

Genny looked at Adam and Silvia, then the bags hanging from the ceiling. She then looked down at Harriot's pleading eyes and simply said:

> "Thank you. My husband gets paid this Friday, and I will pay up when he gets home. Are you still open at seven o'clock?

Adam smiled and just said, "Of course, we are open every day till 9:00 p.m."

ℂ

As anyone who is either fortunate or unfortunate to own their own business knows, a forty-hour week is only about half the hours needed to keep it above water. The only way the Walker family could survive up to present is that they did not have too far to travel to go to work.

Way in the back of the market and toward the right is a well-worn wooden staircase. It is lit by a bare 100-watt lightbulb hanging from the ceiling. This staircase leads to their second-floor two-bedroom apartment. Also in the back of the market, toward the left, is an oversized door. This door opens to the small loading dock through which all inventory is brought in. On the cement loading dock, a two-wheeled dolly is chained to the market's exterior. Next to this is a fire extinguisher mounted on the same wall. The little illustration on the extinguisher stated that it must be tipped completely upside down to expel its water, a fairly new invention.

At this time of his life, when Walt was not helping out at the market, he had one great passion. He loved to play billiards with his friends. In order to keep Walt, who was sixteen, on the straight and narrow, the Walkers made a grand decision.

It was just after dinner one evening, and Silvia was looking around their small living area. Unknown to Adam, she was rearranging the furniture in her mind. Their dining room table was just a small square folding card table. It was set up for each meal, then taken down after each use. Silvia caught Adam's attention and said:

> "Do you think we have room for a full-size
> pool table?"

Adam wanted to respond with a definite *yes* but could not fathom how in the world it would fit. Walt had the excited look of a puppy going for a Sunday walk. With a pathetic and quivering voice, Walt managed to say:

> "Dad, do you really think we can buy a real
> pool table? I mean *a real pool table?*"

Adam surely did not want to disappoint his son, so he looked to his wife to deliver the bad news. Silvia was still looking at the walls and floor area. After a few long, silent minutes, an expression of sheer triumph came across her face. With great authority, she announced her plan:

> "Okay, boys, listen to my idea. We certainly
> do not have enough room to set up our folding
> card table that we use to have our meals *and* at
> the same time have a full-size pool table. We all
> know that. So how about we put away the brown
> folding card table forever. In its place, we might
> be able to fit the pool table. Gentlemen, could

you come up with any idea of how we can use a
pool table for billiards and also a dining table?"

Immediately, Adam took out a small spiral notepad from his
top pocket and started to look for a pencil. Frustrated, he said:

"Why can't I ever find a pencil in this house?
You know our pencils seem to disappear like cotton candy at the county fair."

Taking four steps towards the couch, he sat down and professed:

"When I get to the heavenly pearly gates, I
won't need a pencil, but I'm going to ask Saint
Peter where in tar nations they all went. That is
all I want to know, *where did they all go?*"

Walt found a pencil in the kitchen drawer and quickly sat next to
his dad on the couch presenting him with the elusive writing instrument.
Silvia looked at her men, and a warm glow came over her. How
wonderful that her husband and son were working together to make
a plan. Both added a drawing here or there on the notebook paper,
along with comments one way or another. After a few minutes, they
were ready to deliver their ideas to Silvia. Excitedly, Walt led the presentation to his mother.
"See, we thought if we placed six wooden blocks on the top of
the pool table, we could put a thin wooden oak sheet over the blocks
and the entire table. Covering the whole thing with a table cloth, it
would function as a dining-room table…just like that!"
Silvia had been using a tape measure while the boys were working on their plans. With the findings in her head she explained:

"I have to tell you, guys, a full-size pool table
will have to be partly located in our bay window
as well as in the living room. Otherwise, there
will not be room for the couch."

Both men first looked at the bay window, then at the couch. Walt timidly said, "Do we really need the couch?"

Silvia rolled her pretty blue eyes and said, "Walt, look at my face. What do you think, young man?"

Adam knew they couldn't be happy without a couch, so clearing his throat, he made a manly decision.

"You are right, *lady of the house*. We will put the pool table partly into the bay window."

So, with that decided, the dream plan was on its way. It didn't take too long to acquire a gently used full-size pool table. To get it up the stairs, the legs had to be temporarily removed. Walt got his buddies to help, and Silvia made lemonade to enjoy after the job was done.

For a fussy person, the living area looked unbalanced. The far wall near the steps is their kitchen, the center is their living room the other end is the pool table area. Some called this floor plan a *studio* living area. Many years later, the same arrangement would probably be referred to as *The Open Concept of Living*.

With the family's dining table turning into the billiard table every evening, Silvia and Adam always knew where Walt and his buddies were. They loved to spend hours before supper practicing and improving their billiard skills. In fact, all his four buddies had their own cue sticks, which they would proudly bring with them.

So after school, the neighborhood boys would gather at the market, greet the Walkers who normally were behind the counter, and made it up the back staircase to the family's dwelling. Once upstairs, each boy would carefully take off their white long-sleeve shirts and hang them on wooden clothes hangers found in the corner closet. They then pulled their black suspenders off their shoulders, leaving only their sleeveless undershirts for their top. Their suspenders hung down on either side of their hips.

Taking off their white dress shirts and carefully hanging them up kept them clean for a few more days. In the boy's minds, it also made school seem mysteriously farther away. The boys liked school but could take only so much of reading, writing, and arithmetic studies.

CHAPTER
4

The Mayor

The quaint, little village of Port James boasts of having modest homes in the Victorian style, which blend right along with the downtown commercial buildings. These homes are one family dwellings, but some villagers bring in an occasional boarder. For those tenants renting a third bedroom, some lucky ones also have kitchen privileges. Many times, however, these boarders became part of the family, so to speak. If it worked out with the homeowners, they would also have the use of most rooms, even the parlor, which was normally kept for entertaining special guests.

As Port James grew, it became one of Maine's modest-size seaports. The Maine Merchant Shipping Company built three groupings of rowhouses, each having four attached homes. These homes were very plain, having a flat façade and no porches. If the front door was opened, one could see right through to the back door and into a postage-stamp-size backyard. The dwellings were built for the sailors and shoremen who worked the docks for the shipping company. The Maine Merchant Shipping Company charged very little for rent. It was one benefit extended to the families that were employed by the company. Cans of whitewash was always available from the company if any tenant wanted to freshen up the walls, either inside or out or both.

During a village meeting of residences in the summer of 1951, the honorable mayor, Drake Grimes, requested to be placed on the addenda. His proposal was to have all four entire sections of these rowhouses on South Avenue demolished in stages. His plan was to leave vacant every unit when a resident moved away. Once all four units became completely empty, they would be torn down.

Although very much overweight, the mayor was well-dressed and looked distinguished. While at the speaker's podium in front of the group of taxpayers, he also had quite an intimidating manner. He knew this appearance about himself, and many times, he successfully used that to his advantage. He thought his idea for this part of the village was a "shoo-in." Being one of the few well-to-do families in town, most people felt uncomfortable to question him. After some silence, however, someone asked what would take the place of these homes.

"Well, my fellow citizens, I am planning on purchasing the land...and build a series of strip plazas. It is all the rage now. We need to keep up with the 1950s, my friends, or our little village will be left behind."

Most of those in attendance, including Silvia and Adam who were sitting in the first row, were somewhat leery about his grand plan. A few days before, they heard through the grapevine about the mayor's proposal and felt that this evening's meeting was not one to miss. So that they could attend, they left Walt in charge of the market for a few hours. He might also have to clean up the store before closing for the evening.

The room remained silent until Robert Watercrest, who was bouncing his infant son, Klem, on his knee, asked to speak. Robert volunteered his time extensively at the village's Gray Cliff lighthouse. He had a great affection and respect for history and for buildings with period architecture. He wanted his son to appreciate this as well, so it was important that even somewhat plain historical buildings needed to be preserved. Holding his son in his arms, Robert stood up in order to address the mayor.

"Mayor Grimes, I would like to know who is going to pay for the expensive demolition of these units when they become vacant." Mayor Drake Grimes replied:

"Mr. Watercrest, or may I call you, Robert... in situations like this...which I am sure you all agree is an eyesore...progressive villages gladly pay for their demise."

There was a slight rustle among the gathered residents. Most attendees were whispering among themselves with whom they sat nearby. Mr. Watercrest was still standing, so without hesitation, he offered up his second question.

"Mayor, once the empty land is ready to develop, just how much will this property cost you?"

"Another excellent question, Robert. By the power of your approval here tonight, it would become public domain, but then immediately, I would absorb all the property costs of the land itself since I would have the ownership turned over to me."

Robert was still standing and, therefore, still had the right to continue. However, by this point in time, while looking a bit irate, he politely asked his final question to the mayor.

"Please tell your fellow citizens gathered here tonight exactly how much purchasing this land will cost you."

All eyes were fixed at the mayor who took out his hanky from the front pocket of his three-piece pin-striped suit jacket and wiped his forehead before answering Robert. Mayor Drake Grimes knew the art of debate from his elections, so he also knew how to intimidate his opponent. He regained his composure and aggressively stared right into Robert's steel-blue eyes, stretching his neck over the podium as if to see his opponent better.

"Each parcel tract will cost approximately one dollar."

With this account verbalized, the whole audience of sixty-seven citizens started sixty-seven sidebar comments among themselves. Silvia was just about steaming by this point, but Adam placed his hand on hers to calm her down a little.

By this time, the volume of concerned voices in the room increased dramatically. The mayor could make out very little specific conversations but heard "One dollar? One dollar?" questioned over and over.

In order to quiet the room, Mayor Grimes took out his pocket-knife and banged it repeatedly on the surface of the podium.

Now that he regained everyone's attention, for emphasis, he waited a few moments before continuing.

"Now, good people, let me remind you all one important thing. I will be paying for the cost of building the strip plazas out of my own inherited money...ugh... I mean my money."

The mayor did not expect to have that last statement slip out of his pierced lips. Just about everyone in Port James worked for a living, some families just making ends meet every month. Everyone in the village also knew that the money recently bequeathed to him and his sister was to be split evenly. They also knew the mayor had swindled her and kept it all for himself. To many of the residents of Port James, it just didn't seem fair. The fact was, however, the mayor's proposal could not be stopped. This whole presentation was just a formality. It was a simple and perfect *shoo-in* except for one fatal mistake.

Mayor Drake Grimes thought he would be reelected by a landslide in the next week's vote. The fact was that he did receive quite a few votes. Votes came from numerous people who owed him a favor. Some people voted for him who thought they would benefit from the mayor staying in office. Then there were 236 votes from individuals who, many years ago, had passed from this world to the next. When tabulated, his total vote count was 627. His opponent, Jack Wells, who was twenty years his junior, won the election with 4,584 votes.

So the mayor left office, and the dwellings stayed without being demolished. Some citizens who could not afford a home of their own would still be able to continue living in these units and enjoy their life. They thanked God for giving their families such a nice place along the seacoast to live.

Sherman, Thomas, and Lady Remington

Three miles outside of the village stands an old Greek revival mansion. The front, which faces the road, has two white fluted pillars with Doric column heads that support the second floor. This second floor is basically an architectural triangle. Between the second floor and column heads is well-proportioned dental molding. The whole façade of the home is well-balanced. This stately home was constructed during the mid-1800s using high-quality, native Maine building stone.

When entering the grand foyer, one is greeted by a beautiful ram-horn-shaped staircase at the far end. The foyer is oversized, requiring at least fifteen paces to reach the center where an impressive four-tiered Austrian crystal chandelier hangs overhead. To the right of the grand staircase is the library having entrance pocket doors made of rich-grained mahogany wood. If ever the need arose, these doors could close the library to the rest of the house. The left side of the staircase mirrors the same kind of pocket doors but opens to a formal parlor room where special guests were entertained. A full-concert grand piano takes up a third of this room. Three rows of gray metal folding chairs have been carefully placed, facing the piano in auditorium style.

The ceiling height on the first floor is a twenty-one-feet boasting, beautiful, and ornate plaster molding along the ceiling throughout each room. All the first floors are made of a fourteen-inch-wide tongue and grooved oak pegged boards. Each of these three main rooms have fireplace mantles boasting of black Vermont marble streaked with white quartz crystals. When there is a nice fire in each, they are totally adequate to comfortably warm the entire home. Now that spring has arrived, each fireplace was made spotless of any wood and cinders from winter use. In the back of the fireplace is a one-foot-square door, which opens to the outside. For cleaning purposes, this little door was used so cinders could be swept through to the outside lawn.

In the back of the mansion and out of view, a smaller staircase leads from the kitchen and up to the second and, eventually, the third floors. At one time, this was the domestic's staircase. Using this smaller staircase, the help could work in the kitchen or in the second-floor bedrooms without being seen until it was time to present various meals to the family in the formal dining room.

In its day, this home was a gleaming jewel of the area. It was built for the Forbs family who made their money in lumbering. There were several hired staff who tended every need of the Forbs. They also maintained the gardens and grounds. Not one leaf of hedge row or rose peddle in any of the gardens were ever seen out of place. Today, the home is still spectacular, even though a bit of a shadow of its former self.

The present owner, Lady Remington, is an eccentric lady, Her age is hard to guess. She never leaves her home without makeup or without putting her long black hair up in a bun. During both winter and summer months, she always wears a black blouse with long sleeves. She sometimes completes her attire wearing an off-white flowing scarf, a black mid-length pleated skirt, and an always shiny black silk stockings having a seam in the back. Her preference of house shoes, which she always wears inside, are black leather dress shoes having two-inch heels. The rounded toe of the shoe provides a perfect spot for a small bow.

Unfortunately, Lady Remington had conceded to wearing black leather flats when she wanted to go anywhere. Since she does not own a car and rarely drives one, she uses her heavyweight-woman's Schwinn bicycle with balloon tires to go on all her errands. Wearing two-inch heels while riding her bike would just not work while peddling the three miles into Port James.

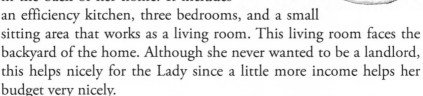

For the past sixteen months, Lady Remington has rented out the third floor, the original servant's area in the back of her home. It includes an efficiency kitchen, three bedrooms, and a small sitting area that works as a living room. This living room faces the backyard of the home. Although she never wanted to be a landlord, this helps nicely for the Lady since a little more income helps her budget very nicely.

The family who rents the back is pleasant enough and are quiet and hardworking. They are members of Our Lord's Lutheran Church and, with their two boys, Thomas and Sherman, attend service each and every Sunday. In fact, the boy's parents sing in Pastor Westman's choir. Lady Remington required anyone renting part of her home to respect it and absolutely must not be heavy drinkers. They also must understand her need for total privacy. This family of four meets all her qualifications. Lady Remington knew her tenant's last name was Tinker but never wasted her time trying to think of what nationality they might be.

She had more important things to do, like learning endless classical piano pieces of Brahms, Bach, Chopin, and Beethoven. All dressed up with her oversized silver jewelry, she enters her parlor in front of the folding metal chairs. With a deep, gracious bow, she acknowledges her imaginary audience that fills her fantasy concert hall. Most of the time, she plays late into the evening. Sometimes she performs so late into the night that she wakes up to find herself bent over the keyboard, her head nested in her crisscrossed arms. Whenever that happens, she stands up and graciously apologizes to her imaginary concert hall audience. Wearing her black flowing dress, and with a most feminine curtesy, she pauses, raises her arms to her audience, then leaves the room, with the applause still continuing only in her mind.

Mr. Tinker, whose first name is George, and his wife, Carmen, enjoy their two perfectly fine boys. Sherman and Thomas hang around together all the time. During the summer months, one pastime of these youngsters was to spy on Lady Remington. They loved it when she went into the basement to wash clothes. She had a wringer washer, the kind that a person could press garments somewhat dry between two rubber rollers mounted above the washer itself. Lady Remington would take the dripping garments out of the washer and feed them between the rollers while she turned the crank with a large handle mounted on the side. The Tinker brothers were totally fascinated with this mechanism and wondered what they will think of next.

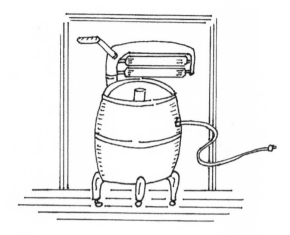

Thomas and Sherman would wait for Lady Remington for what seemed to them hours on end. Being ten and eleven years old, they were surprisingly patient. Sometimes it never paid off, but summer was long, and several wasted afternoons did not matter. One day while waiting for her to come down the cellar steps, boredom set in, so they decided to play in the basement coal bin.

"Hey, Sherman. Let's play king on the mountain on the pile of coal in the coal bin!"

Without much thought of how dirty they would get, they looked one more time for Lady Remington. With her not at all in sight, they scampered off toward the corner of the basement heading to the coal bin pile. There is a twin door to the bin, which keeps the pile from cascading into the rest of the basement. Two small windows in each door allowed the man of the house to view the coal pile to see if it was time to order more coal for fueling the furnace.

Once by the coal bin double doors, Thomas said, "Sherman, lift me up so I can see through the glass!"

Like poorly functioning cheerleaders, Sherman went on all fours, and Thomas used him like a table and looked in. Wobbling back and forth, he said: "About half of the coal is there, about five feet high as I can see. Let's do it!"

And with that, both boys shook hands and cracked open the doors to their black play mountain. It was more fun than either boy could have imagined. In an attempt to ascend the mountain first, each boy made forward strides, chunks of coal slipping pass their shoes. When making it to the top first, either boy sat down on the pile and kicked coal onto the unfortunate brother below. One after the other, Thomas and Sherman made it to the top in just enough time to be pulled down by the other brother's hand. With boyish laughter, they slid back down onto the basement floor, only to crawl back up to the top while being pelleted with coal.

On this particular day, this playtime lasted for most of the morning, but unbeknownst to either boy, the man with the coal delivery truck was arriving. The driver backed the truck down the long drive to the rear side of Lady Remington's home.

After setting the parking brake, he jumped out of the truck while putting on his work gloves. Unhooking a latch on the back of his truck, he swung the shoot around and toward Lady's open basement window. With a quick push of his lever, tons of anthracite coal instantly started to flow down the shoot and through the open window and into the coal bin. Within seconds, the boys were being buried in fresh coal coming from above their heads. Like roaches running through a puddle of whiskey, all drunk and disorientated, the boys made it out of the bin with only seconds to spare.

Sherman and Thomas looked at each other wide-eyed and full of black coal dust. They decided right then and there not to do that again.

On Thursdays of the never-ending hot summer, there was another treat for the boys. At two in the afternoon, when the sun was the hottest, the milkman arrived by truck with his deliveries. The milk was delivered in quart-size glass bottles with paper caps on the top to keep the whole milk from spilling.

Thomas and Sherman watched Terry, the milkman, pick up a twelve-by-twelve-inch block of clear ice from the back of the truck using his huge ice tongs. Using both hands on the tongs, he carried the clear ice block to the back side of the home. He unlatched a small wooden door on the house's stone foundation and shoved the block of ice into the opening. Then he walked back into the truck and placed three milk bottles in his wire handbasket. Once again, he went to the square hole in the foundation and carefully placed the glass bottles of milk on top of the ice, then closed its door. The milk stayed cold enough for Lady Remington to open the box from the kitchen side of the wall and place the glass bottles of milk in her refrigerator.

If the boys could catch the eye of milkman Terry, he always gave them a wink and a smile and said, "Good afternoon, men. I bet you would like to cool your mouths on some ice. You must be quite thirsty out here in the fighting fields."

The boys did not know why he was talking like he was in the military, but they knew what he meant. Following Terry like two duckling chicks with their mother duck, the boys walked in his footsteps back to his truck. Waiting quietly, they watched Terry go into the back of his milk truck. Using his ice pick to chop two small chunks of ice off a large block, he turned and smiled at each boy. Hands outstretched, the boys thanked Terry and received the chunks like it was the best treat ever. Sucking on the pieces of clear ice, they watched Terry jump into the driver's seat of his tan delivery truck. The brothers could hear a ratcheting sound when Terry pulled off the emergency brake and placed the truck into gear. In a few moments, while whistling a little tune, he drove on his way to his next stop down toward the village. Life was good, and as the brothers learned in church, God also is good, caring, and loving.

CHAPTER

6

Changes Here and There

Running the market, Adam and Silvia enjoyed their lives as a working family, but Silvia was still looking for a nice vacation to have with Adam. Between waiting on customers and other various chores, they were just talking about getting away for a short while. Pausing on his broom for a few minutes, Walt felt he was part of his parents' conversation. Walt loved his parents to the ends of the earth but knew that they needed some time together. He also knew that if asked, he would happily run the market in their absence and, of course, carve out some time to play pool with his buddies.

He continued thinking about that while beginning his second task of the day. Tossing out slightly wilted heads of lettuces and overripe bananas, an idea occurred to him. He wanted to tell his dad right away, but by this time, Adam was talking with a salesman about some kind of machine. Walt waited until they shook hands, and the salesman went out the front door with his catalogue and briefcase.

"Hey, Dad. I have an idea that would help run our business more efficiently!"

Adam loved it when his son referred to the market using the word *our*. Looking at his son, Walt had his dad's full attention.

"What do you think if we install a leather strap that holds four or more brass bells onto the market's entrance door? Then whenever a customer comes into our market, we will know it. In fact, it would

46

be loud enough to hear upstairs if anyone of us needs to go to the bathroom or whatever."

"You know, that does sound like a good idea, son. But what about deliveries arriving from the loading dock? If we are upstairs, we would not want to miss any deliveries."

Walt pondered that question for a minute, rubbing his chin with his right hand as if that helped him think better.

"Okay, I've got it! We can install one of those push-button buzzers out at the dock with a sign above it. It could ring in the market as well as upstairs in our apartment. What do you think, Dad? They have one of those buzzers at Beth's Bakery shop."

"Sounds like another great idea. Take some money from the register, and go to Barton's Hardware, and get the items that we will need."

Adam had a flashback to sixteen years ago when he used any excuse to get something at Barton's so he could see Silvia. After they married, he remembered how even when she was sick or tired, Silvia still worked with him day after day. Oh yes, Sundays were kept for rest and the Lord, but he never carved out time for the two of them to go on vacation like Silvia talked about when they were courting. Adam started to talk softly to himself:

> "My lovely wife and I are forty years old, and we have been married now for sixteen whole years. Imagine, sixteen whole years ago! There is no good reason not to indulge in some quality time away with my loving wife. At least for a few days at a time, Walt could easily manage the market just as well as we can. God bless him...he is more than willing to do so. He even said it just today. So for sure, while at the dinner table this evening, we will talk about planning a few days off."

CHAPTER
7

A Questionable Purchase

Standing in front of the kitchen sink, Silvia scraped some cast-off food from each dinner plate into a small paper bag. She stopped for a moment and looked at the discarded food. Both of her men had a good appetite, so there was little waste. During her short moment of reflection, she said a little prayer for those who did not have enough to eat. Meanwhile, Adam and Walt were taking the tablecloth off the pool table, exposing the bare sheet of oak wood. With each of them on either side of the table, they lifted the sheet off and leaned it against the wall. They then removed the six wooden blocks and placed them in the closet near the kitchen area. Walt arranged the billiard balls with the triangle form and placed the cue ball at the other end of the pool table. Adam reached for his cue stick and rubbed some blue chalk on the tip, blowing off the excess. Closing one eye, Walt leaned into the table and was ready to make the opening break with his stick.

Silvia placed the paper bag of table scraps near the drying rack of the sink and then finished up washing and drying the dinner dishes. Her seventy-or-more-year-old dish set was the same one Adam's grandparents, Nataly and Joshua, brought over on the vessel to America. It was not a complete set, but it was nice. Silvia believed it to be Royal Albert china. Each plate had a floral pattern around the edge. Much of the color was worn but not the memories of many enjoyable dinner conservations.

Placing her red cotton drying cloth on top of the dishes, Silvia made an about-face and saw that her two favorite boys were already very emerged in the game.

"Gentlemen…gentlemen! Attention please! Put down those sticks right this instant and try to think of our conservation while at the market a few hours ago. I know it was a long time ago, but thank the good Lord, you both are handsome, but even more important than that, extremely intelligent."

When Silvia talked like an announcer at a baseball game, both knew her well enough to stop what they were doing and listen, giving her their full attention. After father and son exchanged blank expressions with each other several times, Walt's face lit up.

"Oh, I know what you are talking about, Mother! A while back… I can't remember the exact date…a salesman came into the market and left a catalogue with Dad. Isn't that right, dad? Well, he was in again today, and they shook hands. I think they made some sort of deal."

Adam felt like he was falling into a twenty-foot-deep hole but managed to answer his wife directly.

"Uh, yes, Silvia, I cannot wait to tell you what I am thinking of purchasing for the market!"

Silvia rolled her eyes at Adam but said nothing as she analyzed the situation by scrutinizing what seemed to be more blundering sent her way.

After clearing his throat, which was his clever way of adding a few seconds to think on his feet, Adam continued:

> "Darling, you will be happy to know that
> you just might be a *proud* owner of a tube tester!
> I already know where we are going to put it in
> the market."

JAY DIEDRECK

"A tube tester? What the Sam Hill do we need with a tube tester? Will it bring in hordes of customers to look and touch the darn thing? No...don't bother answer that, Adam. Just tell me what it is for."

Adam felt he was more in his element now that he was going to describe the ins and outs of the machine.

"Well, you see, darling, have you noticed that most people these days own both a radio and a television set? If either one is on the fritz, the owner simply unscrews the back panel and takes the tubes out and to our market. This modern unit I just bought looks like a lecture podium. One at a time, people can plug in their radio or television tubes on the side. Mounted on the top is a large meter that can show if their tubes need replacing or not. If our customers want a new tube, there are at least fifty ones inside. There are many sizes, and our customers can be assured that they will find the proper replacement. Isn't that great?"

"Adam, I can see that you are excited about this, but have you given it a thought that Barton's Hardware might have one already? I love you dearly, but..."

Silvia didn't want to dampen her husband's excitement, so she didn't bother finish what she was going to say. She was a little more miffed that they were talking about tube testers instead of discussing vacation plans. How did this happen? Silvia was not used to getting side-railed in conversations.

"So, my Adam dearest, when are you going to talk with the salesman about purchasing this marvelous time-saving device?"

Adam looked down at his knees for some reason, maybe for inspiration. All he saw was that his pants were wearing through his knees, but this was not the best time to tell Silvia about mending them.

"Well, my sweet love, I used my *manly* duty of shielding you from this hard decision and bought it already."

At this statement, Walt could not hold it in any longer. Without any ability to stop, he fell to the floor laughing. With staccato breaths, he repeated his poor father's words over and over:

"Your manly duty? Shielding Mom? Manly duty, *shielding mom*? Dad, you're killing me! Oh, Jesus!"

50

At this, Silvia made a complete change and came to her husband's defense:

> "Don't make fun of your father like that!
> And secondly, don't use the name of our precious
> Savior in that way...ever! Understand, young
> man?"

Walt got up off the floor, tucking in his shirt that got loose from his laughter. Standing now, he stayed as motionless as he could even though he had to swallow a few more pulses of laughter. Mustering as much dignity he could gather, Walt managed to get out a few words to his mother, "Yes, ma'am, I understand. It is my *manly duty* to understand."

And then came another wave of uncontrollable delight that he tried to keep from spurting out his quivering mouth. Poor Walt could hardly breathe at this point. He looked at his mother through watery eyes. He couldn't believe his mother could keep herself from laughing. Not even a crack in her smile. Nothing!

Then without warning, the floodgates opened, and she joined her son's laughter until tears dripped down her cheeks. She dabbed at the collection of tears with her yellow apron. Then after a full minute, she staggered over to her son and husband for a good old family group hug.

They all looked at each other in the huddle, sharing love with their eyes, happy that the tension was over. As they released each other, Silvia sent a round of well-deserved slaps on the top of her men's heads and said:

> "I don't know how much that machine
> costs, but it already gave us much pleasure. I can't
> remember how long it has been since I laughed
> so hard. Now I can't wait to see this magical
> marvel!"

A few days later when the salesman delivered the tester, Adam talked with Walt for a few minutes as to the placement of the new device. Walt thought the machine should be in the back of the market, next to the pet canned food. He said to his father:

> "If we locate it in the back of our market,
> customers may see something else to buy on the
> way through the aisles to the tester."

So, over the next twenty or so years, the tube tester stood in the back and, to Silvia's surprise, was used quite often. Even more of a surprise to her was that over the years, every time Silvia rotated the pet food stock and saw the thing standing against the wall, she burst into uncontainable laughter. From generation to generation, the Walkers worked hard, and it seemed that God gave them a good life as their reward.

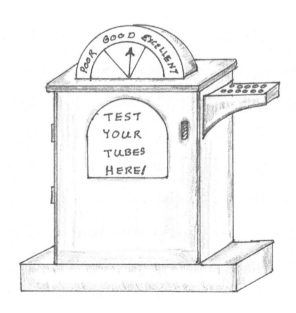

8

Church

All year long, except during summer, Pastor Westman held two traditional services. The first was at 9:00 a.m., the second at 11:00 p.m. By July, just like so many churches, the attendance dropped now that school was out for the summer. Because of the low attendance, only one church service each Sunday was held during this time of year. The summer church service time of 9:45 a.m. was voted on during one of those Lutheran congregational meetings. In order to increase attendance for these meetings, a tasty German dinner of sauerkraut and bratwurst always followed.

Ever since 1920, women in America had the right to vote in elections, but that voting privilege was not extended to women in the Lutheran Church. The men in the church were the only members who could vote on various church considerations. This was certainly a bee in Silvia's bonnet. She would remind church members that over the years, women had played their part or even more to keep the family together. From time to time, Silvia gave little lectures at get-togethers about how women raised their children, managed all aspects of home life, supported their husband's needs, and worked in factories during the war. The workload felt almost insurmountable. She would also say, "And what now? More than thirty years later, they still didn't have a vote in their very own community church?"

One previous pastor before Pastor Westman used to explain it this way:

> "Women do not need to vote. When they go home and discuss church subjects with their husbands, they tell their husbands how to vote anyway."

Several pastors would end it there and say something like, "Now, men, let's get on to more important church business."

Unlike all these previous pastors, Silvia loved Pastor Westman, not just for his powerful sermons, but also for his fairness to women. Oh yes, at first, when he became the new pastor of Our Lord's Lutheran Church, there was always a "honeymoon" period with him and the church membership. Most congregations did not want to offend a new pastor, or worse yet, drive him away in his first few months. There were not enough graduates from church seminary to supply pastors for every Lutheran church.

To become a pastor in the Lutheran Church was a grueling eight years of study. The Hebrew language was studied because the Old Testament was first written in Hebrew. Greek was studied likewise for the New Testament, and German was thrown in the mix since the Lutheran Church had its beginning in Germany. Once a month, many churches still had a service given completely in German. They were surprisingly well attended and enjoyed by those members whose first language was German. Besides the study of these languages, pastoral students learned the Word of God, counseling, sermon writing, liturgy, church music, and much more.

So it was that at his first congregational meeting at this church and during this honeymoon period, Pastor Westman made a strong argument that women should have an equal vote. No sooner did the pastor announce these words during his first church meeting than Silvia stood up clapping wildly showing her total approval. Along with that demonstration of enthusiasm, there was also quite a disgruntled murmur heard in the room, solely amongst the male membership.

SEASIDE JOURNEYS OF FAITH

At this particular meeting, Silvia, moving quickly and smoothly, left the meeting room and hurried to the kitchen where the after-meeting luncheon was being prepared. There she took the lid off the huge pot of simmering sauerkraut, and within half a minute, the aroma filled the meeting room. Banging the metal lid with a wooden spoon, Silvia yelled from the kitchen that the luncheon was now ready. Upon hearing that, a massive flood of men scurried out of the meeting room and into the fellowship hall and the food. It took only a minute for Silvia to make her way back to the meeting room where Pastor Westman and twelve other ladies had remained behind. With no male laypersons present, the amendment for women being able to vote in Our Lord's Lutheran Church passed without opposition. One single vote from Pastor Westman made it happen.

৯০

Now that there was only one summer church service at 9:45 a.m., a little adjustment at the Walker's had to be followed. They were used to the 11:00 a.m. service, and a new shower schedule for the family had to be forged and honored since they only had one bathroom in their upstairs apartment. All this scheduling was worth the time and coordination to have church and God in their lives.

So on the second Sunday of July, Pastor Westman delivered a great sermon of unity to his congregation. Once at the pulpit, he scanned his membership. For that particular day, it was rather warm and muggy. Before the service, the ushers had opened the windows in hopes of letting in an ocean breeze to cool off the sanctuary. Pastor watched both adults and children waving pleated paper fans made from the Sunday's order of worship bulletins. After watching the fans flutter back and forth, Pastor Westman then started his sermon:

> "Dear friends, remember God loves his whole creation, and He loves us all. He is our perfect and loving heavenly Father. He does not love one denomination of Christians more than another..."

Pastor paused for emphases and went on to say, "No matter what Christian denomination a person follows, whether it is Episcopal, Lutheran, Presbyterian, Catholic, Methodist Baptist, Quaker, or any other, we all speak God's word the same, *only with slightly different Christian accents.*"

After the collection, a few more hymns were sung following prayers. Representing almighty God, Pastor Westman turned toward his congregation, and with arms raised toward his people, he said:

"May the Lord bless you and keep you. May
his face shine upon you and be gracious to you.
May He find favor with you and give you peace."

At the back of the church and all decked out with her black dress and blouse and wearing her heels, Lady Remington got ready to leave the sanctuary. She quietly closed her hymnbook and secured it back in its place, then silently made her way to the fellowship hall. She knew how to walk on her tiptoes so her high heels did not make any noise on the slate floor. After the service, there always was a coffee hour in the fellowship hall. The women who organized this coffee hour would also include some punch and homemade cookies so the children would not feel left out.

Once at the fellowship hall, Lady Remington engaged in consuming two large peanut butter cookies. Without making eye contact with anyone, she wiped her mouth on one of the paper napkins that the ladies had spread out on the table like a fan. As singularly as she came, she opened the side door to the outside, where her bicycle waited. Without glancing back to see anyone, she slipped off her heels, exchanged them for her black leather flats, and peddled off to her home, three miles away.

While the adults from church gathered for this fellowship time, Adam was always sought out by the children. They loved to hear about when he was a little boy. Paul, an eighth grader, found his cookie and punch and flagged down Adam. A group of the children gathered around him, finding some space on the rug at the end of the hall to sit. One by one, his audience increased in numbers until there were nine sets of little eyes watching him. The only sound that was heard were the kids munching cookies and drinking punch until Adam started out like he always did. He looked at his gathering and said:

> "God bless you, everyone. Remember, Jesus
> died for you sins so that you will go to heaven to
> be with him when you pass on from this world."

Then looking up toward the ceiling lights and squinting a little to help him think, he entertained the cross-legged children who were sitting on the rug before him. Adam started his story by saying, "It was in the year 1919 way before you, children, were born. In fact, it was thirty-two years ago. Are any of you children thirty-two years old?"

Each child looked around to each other as if one might be that age. All the while, the whole group of kids shook their heads no. Virginia raised her hand completely straight up. From her many hours playing in the sun, the freckles on her little arms were appearing a little more each day. Adam pointed to her and asked:

> "Yes, George, did you want to say something?"

Without the slightest pause, Virginia answered with a little girl giggle, "Mr. Walker, I'm not George. My name is Virginia!"

"And a beautiful name at that! Are you driving a car, and are you attending college, Virginia?"

Even though a little silly, Adam loved to have some fun with the children.

"No, Mr. Walker, I am in second grade, and I can't reach the pedals in my parents' car, but today, I am seven years old!"

With a renewed amazement of how wonderful God was to make innocent and beautiful children for us to guide and instruct, Adam announced:

> "Well then! Stand up, Virginia, and let us
> sing to you 'Happy Birthday!'"

During the chorus of "Happy Birthday," which also ended in "May God Bless you," her older brother presented Virginia with his own cookie as a sweet birthday gift to her, which Virginia took with a smile. Adam continued with the children:

> "Thank you, Virginia, for being born! Now where was I…oh yes it was 1919, and I was eight years old, like some of you. My parents, named Samuel and Beatrice, own a car. But it wasn't like the modern cars of today. It was made by the Stanley Motor Carriage Company. It was deep green in color with spoke wheels, black leather seats, a brass grill, and a wooden steering wheel. And do you know what? The car roof was made of fabric and could be taken off."

Ten-year-old Wayne brightened up and said, "You mean like my dad's new car? It is a 1951 two-door Chevrolet convertible, and it is bright-cherry red!"

"Yes, Wayne, you must be very excited about it! Well, my parents' car was called a Stanley Steamer and was not as sporty as your parent's car. It was really nice looking but a little squarer in shape. Well…anyway, does anyone know what made it go?"

None of the kids knew of anything else except leaded gasoline. That is what the older children guessed, but one younger child named Linda thought it might be a monkey on a large hamster wheel. Most of the sophisticated fifth graders laughed when she suggested it for her guess.

"Well, Linda, that was a good thought, and just for that, I am going to give you another guess."

A little shy now that most of the kids laughed at her, she did not say anything but instead thought for a while. Eventually, with a soft voice, she whispered her answer, "Steam?"

Adam gave her a big smile and a thumbs-up and said, "Yes, Linda! Steam! Kerosene was used to make the fire in a boiler, which made steam that turned the wheels!"

Wayne looked at Linda who was three years younger than him. He thought that in twenty years or so, she would make a nice wife for him. Maybe he will pray about it tonight after he said his "Now I lay me down to sleep" prayer.

Adam said to his spellbound audience, "That isn't the most amazing thing about this car. My mother, Beatrice, and father, Samuel, loved the ocean, and that was their favorite outing. I remember my mom wrapping a raw chicken, raw potatoes, and raw carrots all together in some aluminum foil. By the way, aluminum foil was a brand-new invention back then. Do you know what she did with this package of food? Why, she had my dad place it somewhere under the hood of their car…near the boiler, I think. He did this just before getting the family in the car to leave for the beach. By the time we arrived at the seashore, the meal was fully cooked and steaming hot from the heat of the engine…and oh, so juicy! I can still remember how tasty all of that was! After eating the meal, we ran down to the beach to go swimming in the ocean."

Completely amazed by Adam's childhood story, the children unfolded themselves, stood up again, and thanked Adam. After finding their parents once again, each family started down the church's outside steps to go home.

The two boys, Thomas and Sherman, whose parents rented the back part of Lady Remington's home, said to one another, "That must be why they called the car a Stanley *Steamer*."

While Adam drove back home from church with Silvia sitting next to him and Walt in the back seat, he reminisced about those good times of his youth. Several times throughout the year, his parents would close the market for the whole day and shared the God-given time together.

Now, even before pulling into the alley next to the market, Adam promised to himself that he would definitely spend more time with his lovely wife. They both needed an outing without the daily grind of managing their market.

CHAPTER
9

Nice but Not All Nice

The days of the week went by so fast that Adam couldn't believe it was Sunday again so soon; these seven days just melted away like a sunset over the ocean. However, it was an exciting workweek since he had plans on adding an attraction for children at his corner market. The only thing he needed to do was get Silvia's approval for the purchase. This new acquisition was a carousel-style horse, mounted on a rectangular metal platform. A quarter placed into an attached coin box would electrify the horse, making it move forward and backward. Very few children could resist this marvel. To lure their parents for a quarter, children would climb onto the back of the horse and wave like it was moving. Needless to say, most parents found a quarter and placed it into the box to make it run. For three minutes, the mom or dad watched their child and tried to express excitement to heighten the little one's fun.

Adam knew this latest innovation would be a pleasure for one and all. His thought was to place the mechanical horse in one of two places. It could be located outside in front of the market's window, next to his fruit stand, or just inside the market to the right of the counters. The salesman said that most of his own customers would charge a quarter for the horse ride, but if he wanted, Adam could get a coin box that required only a dime to activate the movement. Even though it would take a month longer to special order a dime box,

Adam wanted it that way. He did not want to disappoint any child whose mother or dad could not afford a whole quarter. The extra time to special order a dime box also gave Adam a few more weeks to think about how to approach Silvia concerning his wonderful purchase.

So here it was, Sunday again, and members were arriving in the church parking lot. Coming out of their cars, they met up with friends, offering each other handshakes, hugs, a pat on the back, or all three. For this Sunday's church service, Silvia and Adam were the official greeters. Standing together in the church's narthex, they were able to exchange pleasantries with everyone as they entered. Looking down into the short line of people, Silvia quietly motioned to her husband.

"Adam, see that boy still outside waiting to come in? He looks so dejected. I wonder what his story is."

"I don't really know, darling, but I know his name is Zinc Bitter."

"Adam, what an awful name. I can't call him that!"

"Well, Silvia, that is his name, and here he comes."

Silvia looked into Zinc's eyes and saw only sadness with no hope for change. The poor child had nice bone structure, broad shoulders, and was almost six feet tall when not slouching over. He was, however, severely underweight or, worse yet, malnourished even to the point of being emaciated. His skin was a sickly pale hue, his fingernails yellow and cracked at the ends. Zinc's movements were ghostlike, and the way he interacted with everyone looked like a frightened dog with his tail between his legs. Silvia couldn't believe a young boy of teenage years could be so downtrodden.

Silvia mustered a smile and said:

"Hi there, Zinc. Good morning and welcome!"

Zinc said nothing but politely extended his bony hand for a congenial handshake. It was weak and lifeless with no emotions. Silvia could not help thinking about all the not-so-perfect fruits and vegetables they routinely threw out at their market. That poor child could benefit by having some of that food to eat and nourish his body.

As soon as Zinc left the narthex and entered the sanctuary, out of his earshot, Silvia whispered to Adam:

"Adam, after church do you think you could talk with that poor lad? Something is dreadfully wrong in his life."

Because Adam and Silvia were greeters, they did not want to miss any late arrivals. They remained at the narthex entrance even while the second stanza of the first hymn was being sung. Since the service had now started, they found a pew in the back of the church, making only a little distraction as they sat down and opened their hymnals to join in the singing. From their viewpoint in the back, they could see everyone who attended the worship service. At several points during church, Adam was given a gentle but wonderful spiritual revelation.

While sitting next to Silvia, he came to understand that worshiping in church is not just an individual religious experience but also, as important, a whole group experience. The individual religious experience for worshippers is praising the Lord from one's heart and praying for forgiveness. The group religious experience is listening to the mass of faithful people repeating the Apostle's and Nicene Creed and the Lord's Prayer and singing hymns. Adam looked around and felt for the first time the Christian family of his church *witnessing to him and each other*. All Adam had to do is look and listen and feel the spirit of God around him.

Adam also watched how members left their pews to go up to the communion railing in front of the altar. Some rose ever so slowly, bones and stiff muscles complaining at every joint. For guidance and balance, some members touched the end of each pew since their eyes did not serve them well anymore. Then there were other souls, like Zinc, still coming to the altar in faith even though their lives were in distress. Without knowing it, they all were witnessing to Adam and each other. As the Holy Communion drew to a close, he had a little tear of thankfulness in his eyes.

A few minutes later, Adam saw his chance to talk with Zinc unfortunately disappear as he watched the poor boy leave church very quickly after the Holy Communion. Zinc knew his father would be drunk again, so he needed to get home before the man woke up. He didn't like his son depending on some invisible god, and after much whiskey, it made him even more upset.

After the church service and the following coffee hour, Adam expected to be pursued by the children once again. This time however, there were only teenagers, including Walt and his buddies, lingering around. The younger children were gathering downstairs to get the name of their next Sunday school teachers for when instruction started back up in September.

Seven of the older boys and girls saw their chance to get Adam's attention and approached him at the cookie-and-punch end of the table.

"Hey, Mr. Walker, can you tell us one of those impossible questions of yours?"

Adam thought for a moment and remembered one that his grandfather Joshua told him. "Okay, put on your thinking caps."

The boys made the gestures of putting something on their head, and the girls gave soft giggles of admiration for them.

"It goes something like this. Three girls were invited to their friend's wedding. They decided to take the bus to Portland where their favorite department store was located on First Street. Once there, they shopped for an hour, looking at many items. They decided to take the escalator to the second floor to find the fine glassware and china section. There, the department store clerk showed them a perfect gift. It was a beautiful cut glass flower vase. Taking it to the register, each girl added ten dollars for the thirty-dollar vase. The nice clerk said their wedding gift could be wrapped at the customer service area toward the rear of the store. After paying for the vase, they walked toward the back, feeling very satisfied with their gift. While their vase was being wrapped, the department store clerk noticed this particular piece of glassware was on sale for twenty-five dollars. She asked the display clerk to find the girls and give them five single dollars. Walking with the money in his hand, the clerk couldn't figure out how to divide five dollars among the three girlfriends. After pausing a moment, he decided to keep two of the dollars for himself and give each girl one dollar each.

"Have I lost any of you kids yet? No? Good! Now here is the problem: each girl paid nine dollars each for the vase, right? Remember, each girl first paid ten dollars, but each were given one dollar back from the clerk. Correct?"

All the teenagers nodded in agreement.

"The clerk kept two dollars, right?" Again, the group of teenagers nodded in agreement.

"Now let's do the math. Three girls payed nine dollars, three times nine is twenty-seven dollars—the total amount the girls paid. The clerk kept two dollars. Twenty-seven dollars plus the two dollars is twenty-nine dollars. What happened to the other dollar?"

The small gathering of teenagers tried to summarize the problem again amongst themselves. The girls certainly thought the boys would figure out what happened to the dollar. Trying to look dignified, the boys offered lame excuses about needing more time. They assured the girls that they would get back to them with the answer.

With that, Adam motioned to his son, and together with Silvia, they went out to the parking lot to find their Buick to go home. Speaking from the back seat of their car, Walt said:

"Hey, Dad, that was great! I didn't think you were so entertaining! You really impressed my buddies, but even better, all the girls were there too! Thanks, Dad! By the way, I noticed there are several pretty girls in our church!"

Riding home in the car, Silvia pulled out her little compact and mirror from her purse to check how her makeup was holding up. With her mirror in her left hand and her lipstick in her right, she applied another coat to her lips. After pressing her lips together, Silvia then placed her compact and mirror back into her purse, turned to Adam, and asked,

"Adam, what was that all about... *you impressed your son?*" After a little silence, Adam replied:

"Oh, that was nothing much. However, I have been meaning to ask you something about a horse purchase I made recently. Now Silvia, love of my life, don't get all upset. It is not a real horse, it is mechanical."

Silvia just rolled her pretty blue eyes, breathed out a long sigh, then told Adam to look out for the cow who was taking her sweet time crossing the road just ahead.

CHAPTER 10

Getting Things in Place

Of all the days of the week, Tuesdays were shipment arrival days and the most exhausting at the market. Adam and Silvia felt blessed to have a son who had a good back for lifting heavy boxes of fresh produce and canned goods. They were equally blessed by God that without even thinking otherwise, Walt was willing to do any and all jobs for the market.

As luck would have it, Walt was able to balance working at the market and his schoolwork. If his parents needed him to sweep the market floor before school, he knew to set up his alarm fifteen minutes earlier to complete the task.

At school one day, while waiting in the lunch line, his buddy Josh had a question for Walt. Lunch at their school cost twenty-five cents and was a nice, hot, well-balanced meal.

"Say, Walt. Why do you help out so much at your parents' market? I mean, your parents don't pay you or anything, right?"

"Well, Josh, why wouldn't I help out? It's my family business, which sustains us. It has been in our family since 1917 when my grandparents opened it. You know, my great-grandparents came by boat from Europe while my great-grandmother was pregnant with my grandfather. He was almost born on the ship! So it is my heritage, my family's livelihood, and all our pride."

Wednesdays, the next day after *shipment arrival days*, were also very busy. Many villagers of Port James relied on the Walkers for home deliveries. If they needed, for a few months or more, some neighbors arranged with Adam or Silvia to have food deliveries for various reasons. Some needed this service after their family had a newborn baby while others needed it when recuperating from an accident or illness. Unfortunately, there were many job-related accidents that occurred at the shipyards. Not able to leave the home while recuperating, these families relied on the food delivery service.

Within several village blocks around Walker's Market are various kinds of living dwellings. Some apartments, like the Walker's, are above businesses located on Third and Fourth Streets and Oak Avenue. There are a few individual vintage homes scattered throughout, which makes for a pleasing balance. On the south side of the village are the rowhouses that were almost leveled by the mayor a few months ago. The vintage homes are mostly owned by Port James's senior population. In total, this is more than half of the entire *downtown* residents. The abundance of older people living near the market did not result from some master plan; it is just the way it evolved in Port James. Nearly every week, many of these older villagers request food home deliveries. Walt would go over the address list with his mother and pack the food in paper bags.

Walt made his deliveries by peddling his bicycle around town. Sometimes even before Walt came down the steps from the apartment to the market, Silvia would already have his bicycle route planned and the paper bags all packed. The grocery list for some were not huge; most of the time, meals were needed for just two people. However, many times, husbands and wives who lost their spouses ate alone but still enjoyed a well-balanced meal using this service. Any customer on the delivery list could be assured that their fruits and vegetables were fresh. Also, older folks felt comfortable knowing Walt would be their delivery boy. After all, whether renting or owning, it was their private sanctuary, and they didn't want deliveries from just any Tom, Dick, or Harry.

Walt was well-known and trusted by all the residents. Some older ladies actually asked Walt to put the groceries in their refrigerator for them. Left over from the earlier generation, some still referred to the refrigerator as the "icebox," which gave Walt a little chuckle. Walt certainly did not mind the extra work of putting things away for them in their kitchen. It usually meant a quarter and occasionally a fifty-cent tip for his extra service.

The only delivery which was a little different from the others was for Lady Remington. First of all, it was three miles away, and Walt always needed to fill his front wire basket and his two side baskets to bring what she needed. Her delivery was this size because she only ordered once each month.

Lady Remington did not have a telephone. She did not see any reason for such a frivolous contraption in her vintage home. Besides, that meant that some nameless male workman from the telephone company would have to come and drill holes in her walls and such. No, not for her, thank you very much!

Besides all that, there was one person she did not want to have call her. It was her horrible ex-husband. Even though she now was in a better place, just the thought of that evil man sometimes made her regress into her very dark times. When those times reoccurred from her memory, she felt like she was trapped in a deep, dark hole in the ground with no way to ever escape.

Without a telephone, Lady let the church help her every first Sunday of the month. On these Sundays, when the ushers passed the collection plate to her, she would place her food delivery order on a folded slip of yellow lined paper along with her church offering. At the end of the service, the collection counters always knew to give the paper to Silvia.

Walt was checking the tire pressure for his bicycle and loading up Lady Remington's order when Silvia went over to him and said:

"Please be careful riding your bike all the way out to Lady Remington's house. Okay? Watch for traffic on West Road. You know they drive much faster than anyone should. Remember, your guardian angel is always with you, but don't tempt your God by being reckless.

SEASIDE JOURNEYS OF FAITH

"Besides, if you get hit by a truck or car and get killed, think of all the babies that want to be born and would never have a chance. They will never become your future children, your grand-children, and on and on. None of them would ever be able to be born! You have quite a respon-sibility to be careful."

After placing the last paper bag of groceries in his bike basket, Walt said:

"Mother, you sound like a Catholic!" Silvia responded. "And what's wrong with that? Lutherans, Baptists, Catholics, Congregationalists, Presbyterian, whatever! Remember, our pastor Westman said we are all Christian—we just speak with different Christian accents."

"Yes, Mother, I will be careful and not temp my God. Now will you do something for me?"

Having felt that he understood her, Silvia answered, "Sure, what is it?"

"I don't mean to be fresh, Mother, but you have been talking about going away for a short trip, just you and Father. How about you stop wishing and just make it happen…and enjoy yourselves. I can take care of the market. Really, I can…you raised no dummy!"

With that, Walt turned his bike toward the street, looked both ways, and pedaled off. Silvia watch her son disappear around the corner and said to herself:

"Out of the mouths of babes…he really knows Adam and I need a vacation.

"No, my son isn't a baby anymore, but there is wisdom in his message. Yes, tonight, Adam and I will plan a few days away. After all, God made a beautiful place with hundreds of miles of coast-

line that we call Maine. I believe God wants us
to enjoy it."

Silvia remembered from her Bible readings of the Psalm 95
verse 5. *The sea is His, and He made it. His hands formed the dry land.*

11

Off and Running

So it was Walt who finally *kicked his parents into gear*. He made them stop talking about it and just do it. The evening before leaving on their adventure, Adam had set the wind-up alarm clock on their night stand for 4:00 a.m. Seven hours later and still dark out, it promptly rang its bell. Still in bed, Adam reached over Silvia and tapped the top of the clock to silence it. Rubbing her sleepy blue eyes, Silvia asked:

"When we get back from our little trip, my
dear, can you promise something for me?"

"Sure, what can I do for you?"

Silvia continued, "You know I don't ask for a lot, right?"

With having more than a little in trepidation in his mind, Adam answered, "Yes, my dearest, you don't ask for much."

"Now remember, you are promising me this even before you know what I want. Adam, could we possibly get one of those new… I think they call them…clock radios from Barton's Hardware? That way, we can awake to beautiful music instead of a loud bell."

Adam had a flashback to the many trips he made as a youth to Barton's Hardware Store, only hoping to see the gorgeous, head-strong Silvia. The woman of his dreams. That was sixteen years ago.

Could it really be that long? Now, still in their bed, he was looking at her and falling in love all over again. *Gosh*, Adam thought, *she is so pretty, even in the morning and just after waking up.*

Adam wanted the memory to last forever—it felt so good in his soul—but as it faded, he replied:

"Of course, we can get a clock radio. Anything for you!"

Adam and Silvia then scooted around their bedroom, placing last-minute things in their luggage. Maybe it was the early hour, but except for the creaking of the hardwood floor from beneath their bare feet, they did not make a sound in their room. Then with a little twinkle in his eye, Adam broke the early morning silence:

"Hey, Silvia, I have been meaning to tell you but haven't had the chance. Remember the nice couple next door to us who just moved in?"

In a rowhouse, *next door* means that there is no outside space between the two individual homes. The Walker's home shared the same wall of their bathroom with the bathroom *next door*. So on one side of the bathroom wall was the Walker's shower in their apartment, and on the other side of the wall was the shower in their neighbor's apartment.

Silvia answered, "Oh yes, that is Marie and Alfonso. Thank goodness that they seem to be a nice young couple. I mean, for us living so close to them, it is a true blessing."

Adam had Silvia's attention. "Yes, that's right...do you think Marie is pretty?"

Silvia looked at her husband who was trying with all his might to look nonchalant, but it wasn't working. Putting her rolled-up nylon stockings into her suitcase, she entertained his question with a simple question of her own. She looked at him and asked, "Adam, where are you going with this?"

"Oh, nowhere, darling. I just wanted you to know that I showered with Marie every morning last week."

Adam could never get a *one up* on his wife, so this felt great to him. "Adam, what in God's creation are you talking about?"

"Well, it turns out that every morning, her shower schedule and mine are the same. Just like clockwork, while I'm soaping up, I hear her turning on her shower on the other side of our bathroom wall. While showering, she sings the beautiful aria from Bizet's opera, *Carmen*. You know, that is a famous French opera."

"Yes, I know *Carmen* is a French opera, my dearest."

"Well, Silvia, are you jealous?"

Placing both hands on her hips, Silvia answered curtly, "Of course, I am. Imagine my husband being serenaded by what he thinks is a pretty lady…in the shower, no less!"

Adam was enjoying this playfulness which was happening between him and Silvia. He decided to continue his true-life account:

"One thing, however, two mornings ago, she was performing her aria while taking *a bath, not a shower*."

"I'm afraid to ask, but here it goes. Adam, dearest, how do you know that she was *bathing, not showering*?"

"Oh, I thought you would never ask. Us experts can tell the difference by the sound of the running water. For the discriminating ear, the sound of a shower is quite different than a tub being filled."

Rolling her pretty eyes, Silvia said, "I see *Mr. Water Expert*!"

"However, Silvia, what perplexes me is that I could also tell she was smoking a cigarette in between singing. The slightest, little scent of her cigarette came through the wall into our shower."

With sarcasm in her voice, Silvia asked, "Hum… I see, and, Adam, was it a regular or a filter-tip cigarette?"

Now it was Silvia who had Adam feeling a little on the run, so to speak. She took a quick look at what Adam was doing and said:

"Adam, don't pack those trousers on our trip! They are dirty. Find some clean ones in your closet. While we are away, we don't want to waste time going to some laundromat! Be sure you also pack enough clean socks."

Somehow, Adam sensed that she was not done with her part of this early morning playfulness.

"Adam, I must let you in on some *top-secret* knowledge that I have obtained about our new neighbors. Yes, you're right, Marie and Alfonso moved in a week ago, but Marie had to go back to Boston right after arriving to finish the last of their packing. Adam, you have been showering with—and being serenaded by—*Alfonso, not Marie*…and he was smoking a cigar, not a cigarette."

Glancing at the bedroom clock, without cracking a smile, she turned to Adam, who still had his socks in both of his hands and looking dumfounded.

"Adam, with that additional information you now possess, will you let *me* take my shower? You see, Adam, dearest, I think Alfonso is about ready to take *his* shower, and now it is time for *my* shower… or should I say *our* shower."

Placing his socks in the luggage, he picked up his gold pocket watch and started winding it. He thought for only a few seconds and said:

"Very funny… I am coming with you, Silvia."

"Not so fast, big guy. There is not enough room for two, let alone three of us in our bathroom."

With that, Adam took some tank-top undershirts from his dresser and placed them in their luggage. He would have felt completely deflated except for one thing. As he watched his wife walk toward the bathroom door without turning around, she gave that adorable little wave with her fingertips. With that single gesture, he knew they were going to have a *great* time.

By this hour, Walt was up and moving around the living area. He had already changed the pool table into the dining table and had put out their breakfast plates. In the center, he arranged sweet rolls on a china serving platter and had coffee brewing next to the stove on the kitchen side of their apartment.

Sitting down to eat with Walt, Silvia and Adam hurried through breakfast. When they finished, they made one last look around their bedroom and went downstairs, carrying their luggage in hand. With Silvia in the lead, they walked through the market, to the back loading dock where their car was parked. Adam opened the trunk and placed both suitcases in, then quickly went around to Silvia who was waiting at the passenger door. With a gracious bow before his wife, Adam unlocked her door with his key and opened it for her. Silvia paused for a moment and, with a soft touch of her hand to his cheek, whispered to Adam:

"You are my man, my hardworking man whom I love to the ends of the earth. I can't ever think of anything more perfect than to take off with you for a few days. *I truly love you.*"

As needless as it may be, both of them were a little nervous about leaving the market for a few days. As they rolled down their windows from the front seat of their Buick, they waved back at their son. Walt was standing outside at the loading dock next to the two-wheeled dolly, one hand on the fire extinguisher and the other waving good-bye. He was sporting his beige cotton smock, looking confident and truly happy for them. Yes, God has blessed Adam and Silvia.

12

A Remarkable Stop

It was a beautiful July day and a perfect start for a runaway trip. Once on the road, heading south to Ogunquit a few hours away, Adam and Silvia felt like lovers on a date again. This was a glorious feeling they did not partake of for over sixteen years. Traveling the coastal route along the miles of hills and turns, every few miles, they went through one lovely village after another. With car windows fully rolled down, they cruised through seaside towns of Freeport, Falmouth, Cape Elizabeth, Old Orchard Beach, Biddeford, and Kennebunkport. Pointing out her open car window, Silvia said:

> "Adam, just ahead on the side of the road are some of those clever advertising signs for *smooth shave*. Can you slow down a little so I can read them as we go by each one? Let's see, I'll read them out loud…here they come:
> "He dated Margie
> "He dated Sally
> "The one called Honey
> "Spent all his money…
> "Smooth Shave."

"Adam, just what kind of guy thinks of those?"

"Well, darling, I have no idea, but I was just thinking of something else."

Silvia looked across at Adam, her pretty ocean-blue eyes sparkling with pleasure. "Oh really, and what was that?"

"I was thinking about the word *under*. It's kind of odd, Silvia, someone can under*stand*, but no one can under*sit*. A candidate can be an under*dog* but never an under*cat*. A woman can go to a party and be under*dressed*, but a man can never go to a party and be under*panted*."

"Ha! Yes, Adam, and how about someone can under*go* brain surgery, but they can't under*come* surgery. Maybe they cannot get *under* something, but they can get *over* something, like over*come* surgery... Oh boy, I think I am mixed up! I am glad you are driving and not me."

The traffic flow started to slow down a little as they approached Kennebunkport. As Adam downshifted the car into second gear, Silvia was the first to see that just ahead a fireman's carnival was in full swing.

"Oh, honey, since we are here, let's see if we can find parking to enjoy a few hours at the carnival!"

Luckily, there were plenty of parking spots left at the congregational church across the street from the Ferris wheel. A man with a big smile was holding a sign that read, "Free Parking, Goodwill Donations Accepted." Young teenage girls wearing small shorts were waving cars up to the sign, then toward the parking lot.

Adam maneuvered the car up to the girls who then started jumping up and down in front of the sign. He retrieved a dollar from the sun visor and gave it to them. As if they never saw a whole dollar before, with big, beautiful eyes and smiles, all three yelled, "Thank you!" and rang a loud dinner bell several times for the people in the next car to hear.

While Adam took the next parking space in the lot, Silvia said, "Now those girls know how to market! Okay...first, let's head right to the games of chance! Maybe you can win something for your woman, you handsome dude! But please don't forget my cotton candy and powdered sugar funnel cake with strawberries!"

The happy couple got out of the car and crossed the road to the fair grounds. As they walked, Silvia captured Adam's slight aroma of aftershave. It was just enough, not overpowering. Gosh, she thought, this trip was already so much fun. Playing with her ponytail as they went along she said:

"Hey, Adam, look over there in that tent—it's the balloon popping game!"

Still walking hand in hand, except when she was skipping ahead of Adam, Silvia stopped at the balloon game tent. Checking out the rules, she started to assess Adam's chance at winning a stuff doll for her.

There was a young father that had a bunch of darts in his hands. Each dart cost him ten cents. One at a time, he leaned over the counter and launched a dart at one of the balloons that were arranged on a board at the far end of the booth. Try as he might, each time, he missed popping a balloon. Silvia saw that he was just hoping to win a prize for his five-year-old daughter who was patiently standing next to him. Painfully, one by one, his remaining bunch of darts became fewer and fewer. Not even one of his darts popped a balloon. To win any kind of prize, he had to pop three balloons in succession.

Adam caught up with Silvia, and it took no time at all to figure the very same thing. Here was a frustrated father trying his best to be a hero for his child but not getting very far. When the father had only three darts left, Adam paid for three darts for himself. Standing right next to the father, Adam whispered to him to shoot his dart at the exact same time as he did.

With an understanding nod, the father then shot his dart, and Adam threw his. Of the two, only one dart found its target and popped the balloon with a bang. Again, at the same time, the two men shot the second, then the third dart. Right in a row, three balloons were hit. The man at the booth unlatched a doll, then reached across the counter, and presented it to the little girl. It was just what she was hoping for—a bright-yellow stuffed duck with an orange fluffy bill. His daughter exhaled with a "wow!" and hugged her doll while wiggling her body back and forth. The father looked at his big, brown-eyed daughter who couldn't stop smiling. At this point, she was overflowing with admiration for her dad. The father turned to Adam and whispered:

> "I know every one of those three darts were
> yours, and you know that my daughter thought
> they were mine. I thank you, sir, and God bless
> you and your family."

Shaking Adam's hand, then deciding to also hug him, the father continued:

"It's been one month since my little girl lost her mom to a lung infection. Nothing can replace her, but you made our day today. Thanks again."

"Oh, it was nothing, but please know that my wife and I will pray for you and your daughter. What is your name and your daughter's name, my friend?"

Looking at both Adam and Silvia, the father took his little daughter's hand and said:

> "My name is Abe, and this is Francis. Can
> you say *hi* to these nice people?"

Francis shyly said, "Hello," then, with both of her little hands, hugged and kissed her duck on its bill. After that, Francis looked at Silvia and Adam and stated:

> "I am going to take my duck everywhere
> because my mom can't come with us anymore.
> She is in heaven."

Adam placed his hand on Abe's shoulder and said:

> "I can see you are a good father, and Francis
> is a precious daughter. Like I said, please know

that every night my wife and I will pray for you both. Remember, our loving Creator is always with you and will help you through these hard times. God bless."

Silvia looked at her own hero. She was bursting with pride and affection for what her husband had just done. With the cutest wink ever, she promised, "Adam, you are wonderful, and you will get *your* prize tonight!"

Feeling as fulfilled as a man can be, Adam said, "My dear Silvia, whatever do you mean? Wait, don't answer that question just yet."

Once again, Adam took her hand in his. This time, he rushed with her as fast as his forty-plus-year-old legs could take him straight to the Ferris wheel. They met the attendant and gave him their tickets. He placed the tickets in a box and raised the security bar on the Ferris wheel seat so the two could sit. Once in their seats and moving upward into the sky, Silvia kissed Adam passionately during the entire ride.

Adam couldn't help but think that this has been the best money he spent in years. It was even better than buying a new expensive cue stick for playing pool. This was another purchase he happened to forget to tell Silvia.

The ride slowed down, and eventually, the Ferris wheel and their chair came to a stop at the boarding ramp. The operator lifted the guard bar and swung it open for them. Running off the ramp of the Ferris wheel like little children, Adam asked Silvia if they could now go to the dairy cow judging tent.

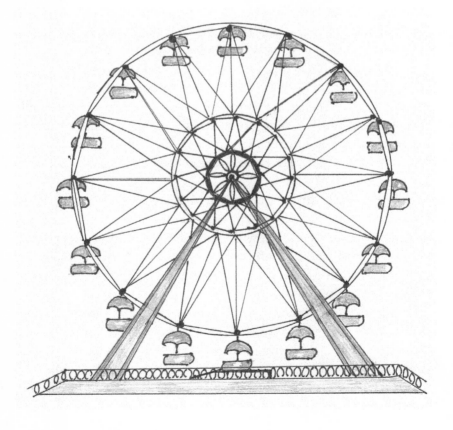

"Adam, I am putty in your hands, lead the way!"

The dairy cow tent was huge, being able to easily house thirty heads of cows, the judging area, and bleachers for the spectators. Along the perimeter were stalls where the cows were fed, brushed, and cleaned. Adam led Silvia by the hand up to the top of the bleachers for viewing and waited for the next cow to be judged. Within a few minutes, a man wearing blue jeans, a red checkered flannel shirt, and a black Texas-style hat stepped up on a platform near the bleachers and took a microphone from its stand.

After viewing the cow from his vantage point, the judge asked the owner to walk her around in the showing circle. With considerable amount of experience in raising cattle, he could give a critical look and assessment for every aspect of this specimen. After making some notes in his book with his pencil, he pointed to the cow but faced the spectators. Meticulously, he began to announce his decision. Novice to all this, but eager to learn, Silvia and Adam sat up straight in their wooden bleachers to listen intently to his words.

"After carefully analyzing this week's class of Holsteins, I place this heifer in the top ten out of thirty. Her shoulders blend smoothly into the body and is feminine throughout the head and neck. Equally important, she displays straightness across her top and ample strength in her loins. She is squarer than most in the rump and walks with more ease. I do not fail to recognize that she has a desirable angle to the rear foot."

At this point in his evaluation, the judge looked again at his notes, took off his hat, and briefly rubbed his forehead with the tip of his thumb. In the bleachers, with amazed looks on their faces, Silvia and Adam just stared each other. Adam could not keep from showing his little adolescent kind of smile while Silvia did not know what to think. Then the judge continued:

"Upon further examination, I prefer this heifer mostly because she exhibits great superiority in udder quality and capacity and shows a youthful udder appearance. Therefore, all things considered, I place her a respectable third."

After hearing this, Silvia couldn't keep back her comment any longer.

"Third? Really? Third? Did you hear that Adam? After all of that, she places third? What's with that, Adam? The cowboy judge, who I might add is *a man*, said the cow has a superior udder! Did you see how smooth and youthful her udder was? For crying out in a bucket! He places her in third? Really? Third? What the heck, Adam! Third?"

Working themselves down from the top of the bleachers, Adam did not know how to respond to his wife. He did manage to say, "I would have placed her second, maybe even first!"

Silvia felt she had to have the last word, so she answered, "Adam, first you are a water expert concerning our shower—now you are a cow judging expert? Just don't you dare judge me like that!"

Even though at first being pretty serious, now she was really making a playful game of this with Adam. Looking into his eyes and waiting for his response, she did not know what he would come back with.

"Oh, Silvia, my love, I would never judge you like that. My reasoning is that out of every female, I have encountered, I rate you as a perfect specimen."

Rolling her beautiful ocean-blue eyes, Silvia just answered, "Adam, you promised me some cotton candy."

After reaching the bottom of the bleachers, most of the spectators headed outside to see what was in the next exhibition tent. Adam and Silvia walked with the rest of the folks along the tent's inside perimeter. Eventually, they again came across the individual stalls where the cows were standing and eating straw. If a cow earned a colored ribbon, it was pinned on the one of the wooden posts of the stall as a show of pride and accomplishment for the owner.

Silvia paused next to one stall, where several young farm girls were talking and laughing with each other. She noticed a sleeping bag that was obviously slept in. It was perched on top of a bale of straw. Silvia knew if she did not ask the question that was rolling around in her head, she would later regret not knowing the answer.

"Excuse me, ladies, but what is that beige sleeping bag doing on top of the straw bale?"

The small group of three stopped conversing with each other and looked her way. One farm girl, who was wearing a red-and-white-checkered blouse having three quarter sleeves, blue jeans, and scuffed cowboy boots, spoke up. She had the cutest Southern accent. Her sweet face and long arms were sun-kissed, and she saw the world through her beautiful, sparkling hazel eyes.

"Why hello, ma'am! That is my cow and my sleeping bag. We all sleep next to our animals during the fair. We need to stay with our cows all the time."

Then in front of the other two dairy farm girls, she showed an amazing, innocent love for her animal and the love of her family's farming livelihood. Originally from the South, she was born into this way of life. With no hesitation, she put her hands on either side of her cow's head and kissed her wet, slippery black nose. The other two farm girls did not laugh or giggle. This affection was purely natural and wholesome. Dairy farming, their cows, and long working hours were their way of life, and it was a good one.

Walking back to their car, Silvia completely forgot about her cotton candy. Instead, she pondered what she experienced that day. As Adam backed the car from the parking spot, Silvia said to him:

"Adam, have you noticed that in our lives, God gives us both talents *and* opportunities? It is up to us to nurture these gifts even if it means performing hard work...and it always does. We need to do our very best because these gifts of talents and opportunities are from our Creator."

Silvia offered up a silent prayer for God to bless these dairy farm girls and their families who live and work in agriculture all over our nation. She asked God to bless *all* those who labor, whether in stores, factories, farms, schools, churches, and every other occupation. Silvia felt that everyone who goes to work day after day deserves God's blessings.

Silvia had one more revelation. Hard work, itself, is also God's gift to us.

After a short drive, just off the side of the road, they came across an ice cream stand. Silvia asked Adam to pull into its small parking area.

"Adam, you promised me some cotton candy. Since we didn't get any, let's have some dessert here! Adam parked next to the sign listing the thirty-four different flavors. After pondering their selection, Adam jumped out and around the front of their Buick, unlocking the passenger car door and opened it for Silvia. Before walking up to the ice cream stand window, she purposefully brushed close to her husband and said, "Adam, thank you for taking me away today… and thank you for being such a hard worker your entire life, I truly love you."

A Vacation to Remember

Being admired by the love of his life, Adam felt blessed by God and on top of the world. As he manicured his ice cream cone with his tongue, he looked over at Silvia doing the exact thing. Adam thought there was something unusually seductive in the care she gave her dessert with her tongue.

"Adam, just what are you up to in that mind of yours? Do you wish you had gotten the mint chocolate chip instead of just plain vanilla?" Reaching over to give Adam a little taste, she said:

"Hey, big guy! Don't take too much, just a little lick. You have your own to take care of. While you at it, let me have a little vanilla of yours."

They exchanged each other's a few times, enjoying their closeness that comes from sharing. Once they finished their cones, Adam backed the car from the parking spot and reentered onto the highway. Silvia slid across the bench seat a little closer to her soul mate, feeling the warmth of his shoulder next to hers. From time to time, Silvia enjoyed pointing out nearly everything she saw. Soon, they were entering the little village of Ogunquit.

"Oh, look, dear, this area is so beautiful! This village actually has a small movie theatre, and over there is the library, but it looks just like a small gray stone castle! How charming! I know you are concentrating on driving, but can you see all the shops and restaurants along the streets?"

The name *Ogunquit*, translated from the Abenaki language, means "a beautiful place by the sea," and it truly is. The Abenaki were Native American Indians who lived in Maine and farther north into Canada. Ogunquit was settled in the year 1641 and was a shipbuilding village for schooners in 1686.

Studying the map, Silvia said, "Let's see if we can find our inn. It is located near where they call the Marginal Way. Let me unfold this road map and see if I can find it. Oh yes, looking at the map, I see that it is just on the southern side of town."

Within moments, the two explorers were pulling into the crushed stone parking lot of Ocean Visit Inn. This inn is a cluster of what looks like many individual Victorian cottages having rounded turrets and open balconies. Each generous balcony either faces the beautiful grounds of flowering hedges and rose hips or breathtaking views of the ocean.

Once parked, Silvia and Adam gathered their luggage from the trunk of the car and strolled up the brick walkway, which was lined on both sides with red geraniums. As they entered the quaint lobby area of the inn, the receptionist at the counter greeted them. A huge stone fireplace was on the left, and a bank of windows on the right gave a 180-degree view of the ocean.

"Hello there, my name is Judy. May I help you?"

Silvia let her man answer the nice girl.

"Why, yes, you certainly may. We are the Walkers and have reservations to stay here for three nights."

"Splendid, and welcome! I can help you check in. Have you ever stayed with us before?"

This time, Silvia answered with a smile as she placed her luggage down on the wide planked hardwood floor.

"No, we haven't stayed here before, but I have a feeling we will be coming back. This place is beautiful!"

Judy responded with a smile and said:

"Thank you, and I know you will enjoy your ocean-view room. Let's see...oh nice, your room is 218, so it is on our second floor.

Once we have the paperwork filled out, you can be on your way. I see from the maid's notes here that the room is already made up and ready for your stay."

Adam completed the short registration, then took the keys Judy placed on the counter in front of him. He had a smile on his face when he saw the keyring had a silver sailboat charm attached with the keys.

"By the way, Mr. and Mrs. Walker, breakfast is in the front room. It is a hardy buffet, so come hungry anytime from 6:30 a.m. to 9:00 a.m. If you come before 7:00 a.m., you will see the sunrise through the windows. I start working here early enough to enjoy it every morning. The colors are almost always orange and yellow in the sky and are also reflected in the ocean surf. Sometimes if the sand is wet enough, it will catch these spectacular colors too. I guess you can tell I love it here! I know you will enjoy your visit with us! See the staircase behind me to your right?"

Both Adam and Silvia looked toward the direction that she motioned to with her arm outstretched. Just before the staircase was a French provincial end table that had a glass vase filled with beautiful miniature sunflowers.

"You can use that one to get to the second floor. Your room is halfway down the hall. We don't have an elevator. By the way, I, or someone else, will always be here at the desk if you have any questions. Later on, please come and see me... I can recommend some great local restaurants."

Silvia couldn't wait for Adam who was now carrying both of their luggage bags. Skipping excitingly a few steps ahead of Adam, she stopped and gave that delightful, seductive finger wave that only Adam could see. By now, she was famous for this wave, even though she kept it for only her husband. Adam watched as his heart rate quickened just a little. For some reason, he did not notice that Silvia had pulled her shiny black hair back into a single ponytail. He wondered when she did that. Was it just before going on the Ferris wheel? Maybe. Climbing the stairs to the second floor, it swished back and forth with every movement she made. He loved that. Gosh, she was adorable.

Silvia quickly found the room and opened the door for both of them to enter. Their suite was more pleasing than both Silvia and Adam expected.

"Adam… Adam, look! We have both an outside porch, and over there is a rounded room. That must be part of the turret that you can see from outside. Adam, we have our own turret! I think the size of these rooms combined are larger than our apartment in Port James!"

Prancing from one end of a room to another, she said, "Look here! In the hall is a little refrigerator just for our use. Later on this evening, we can buy some wine or some locally brewed beer and chill it just for us!"

After looking at the bedroom and bath, they both met on the outside porch. It was narrow but had two light-blue Adirondack chairs that were surprisingly comfortable. After a few minutes, both of them became aware of some people below, walking along a path that followed the coastline. Pointing down to the strolling people, and turning to Adam, she said:

"Adam, we still have a few hours of light left.
Can we go down and see what that is about?"

"Of course, my dear."

Taking a deep breath, Adam pretended that he was going to jump from the second-story balcony to the grass lawn. Grabbing his shirt tail, Silvia said playfully:

"For heaven's sake, Adam, don't break a leg
doing something stupid…at least wait until we
are back home."

The strolling path is one mile long and is called Marginal Way. Even though Ogunquit is in Southern Maine, the coast is wild with cliffs and surf that rivals any other along the state's entire coast.

It took only a few minutes for them to make their way downstairs and back through the lobby. Walking past the counter, Judy looked up and said, "Have a nice evening, Mr. and Mrs. Walker!"

Silvia looked at Adam and said, "Honey, I already love it here, and that sweet girl even remembered our names!"

Once outside, they headed onto the path, joining a few other families. Silvia grabbed Adam's hand and just stood facing the water for a while, taking in the indescribable coastal panorama.

"Adam, I had no idea that this area is so breathtaking! The surf seems so very much alive! Did you see that last wave crashing into those cliffs? Just smell that salty air! There is nothing quite like ocean air for the soul."

As they walked along hand in hand, they were unaware that another treat was waiting for them just around the curve. Perkin's Cove is nestled at the end of the path where they were walking along. This village has a very small harbor inlet with a nice cluster of shops and restaurants. The cove has one narrow street, and when window-shopping, visitors can see the ocean on their left side and the harbor to their right.

Silvia and Adam decided to eat at a restaurant right in Perkin's Cove that served steamed lobster. Silvia opened the screen door to the eatery and peered in. To the left were the kitchen staff behind the counter. Along the wall was a huge stainless steel tank of ocean water with live lobsters piled three deep. Hanging from a chain was a chalkboard displaying its menu. Adam stood just behind her and read the menu out loud.

"Let's see, fresh-steamed lobster, boiled potatoes with butter, corn on the cob, rolls, coleslaw…it all sound great! Besides lobster, there is also fresh-caught local fish. Oh, and I see there is also New England clam chowder listed on the board."

At that point, a fellow named Oskar, who was working behind the counter, said to them and several other customers:

"The chowder is white, thick, and very tasty." Adding to that, he said, "With every bowl of chowder, there are plenty of clams, which, I might add, are very tender… I shucked them this morning. Have any of you here ever had our chowder before?"

Adam said that they hadn't the pleasure.

"Well, our New England clam chowder that we serve here is the very best-tasting chowder you will ever find. You will see that we make it so thick you could stick a spoon up straight in the chowder, and it would take its time to tilt over to the side of the bowl. If you can find another chowder that is better tasting, tell me how much you paid for it, and I will give you that much. To tell you the truth, in my fourteen years of working here, I have never had to pay anyone!"

Oskar looked directly at both of them and asked, "Will that be two bowls or one bowl with two spoons? Two bowls? Great, you won't regret it. By the way, have you ever tasted our homemade cheesecake or ice cream?"

After placing their lobster order along with two bowls of their famous chowder, Oskar told them to find any table they wanted to sit at for their meal. They walked down three steps to the main dining area and easily found a small, round table overlooking the harbor. They sat across from each other with contentment in their souls.

"Silvia, you look so ravishing this evening, yes, just stunning!"

"Oh, Adam, I was going to say something funny like, *Are you sure I look like this only because I am a little flushed from our walk?* But I will accept your complement joyfully, knowing you are a self-proclaimed *expert* in judging women."

Their meal was simple, and Oskar was truly right about the chowder. It was magnificent. The lobster couldn't be any more fresh and flavorful. The lobster meat even had a sweetness to it. After dunking each piece into a white porcelain cup of drawn butter, both of them rolled their eyes and savored each delightful morsel. When the lobster was all gone, Adam used the remaining drawn butter for his rolls. Silvia rolled her pretty eyes, then noticed a little drip of butter on his chin. She took her napkin from her lap, reached over, and tenderly wiped the butter off his face for him.

"Adam, dearest, I am so full, but we really should try their homemade ice cream. Is it too much to have two ice creams each in one single day?"

Without waiting for Adam to answer, she got up from their table and said, "Let's see what flavors they have."

Before taking the footpath back to the Ocean Visit Inn, they strolled along the inlet using their ice cream cones in their hands like pointers. Various types and sizes of watercraft were moored, but other boats on the water passed them while leaving the cove to take an excursion before dusk arrived.

Returning back to the inn along Marginal Way gave them the same pleasure as when walking in the opposite direction. Every scene looked new, and at this time, the yellow and orange glow from the setting sun made a beautiful backdrop. Rolls of surf splashed onto the rocks, sending saltwater sprays skyward before rolling back into the ocean for another encore performance.

When they walked closer to the inn, Silvia and Adam were delighted by the warm glow of footlights along the path to the gardens. All around them and above them, the rooms in the inn casted golden glows of light from their balconies. Silvia could just make out the silhouettes of a few other couples looking toward the ocean for one last glimpse before dark.

Once inside the inn, walking through the lobby, they were hoping to see Judy, but she had already gone home. Now working at the counter, an older gentleman caught their eye as they passed and asked:

"How was Perkin's Cove? And how was the chowder? Did Oskar get you to buy a bowl of his famous brew?"

Adam said, "He did, and the chowder was the best we have ever had the pleasure to enjoy. The lobster was fantastic too!"

They went up the staircase, then to their room. Once inside, Adam decided to give Walt a phone call to see how he was managing his first day alone at the market. In the bay window area was a black telephone sitting on a little table. He picked up the receiver and dialed their home.

Back in Port James, Walt closed the market just a few minutes before the desk phone rang. He had fully intended to play some billiards with his buddies but was totally exhausted by 10:00 p.m.

"Hi, Dad, yes, everything went really well, but I can hardly see straight because I am so tired. My feet are killing me...no really!"

Adam looked at Silvia who was combing out her tangles. When her hair became wet, it tended to curl in ringlets at the end. This time, it was from the ocean breeze. Turning around toward her husband, she tried to understand what Walt was telling his dad. With some patience, she continued a few more finishing brushstrokes through her hair and decided to just wait until he hung up to hear the story from Adam.

"So, Dad, I was thinking. How about we hire those Tinker boys, Thomas and Sherman, to do some of the nearby grocery deliveries on Thursdays? They both have bicycles and come from a nice family. I don't know what the boys would do all summer long. Maybe this would break up the boredom for them."

Adam loved the way Walt was taking the *bull by the horns* and was becoming a real partner in the business.

"Walt, that sounds like a good idea. Before talking to the boys about this, be sure to work it out with their parents first. What were you thinking about paying per hour?"

"Let's see, Dad. How about starting them out with seventy-five cents each? Yesterday, I saw in the newspaper that the current minimum wage for 1951 is that amount. Later, if things work out, we can give them a ten-cent increase."

Adam agreed with his son and closed the conversation with, "We love you, Walt…just go for it."

"Bye, bye, Dad, I love you too, and tell Mom I love her too."

Adam hung up the telephone and went out to Silvia who was now on the porch. There they stood, arm in arm, looking up into the star-filled night sky. They drank in the moist ocean breeze and the love they had for each other. Adam moved to her backside and started to gently message her shoulders and then followed the gentle curve in her back with his fingertips. The many years of lifting produce boxes in the market kept her muscles firm and delightfully curvy.

Silvia did not want this moment to ever end. Adam's touch on her arched back gave her delightful shivers up and down her firm, smooth body. Then in their shared silence, God decided to deliver a dynamic moment of His own creation. Faintly over the ocean and high in the sky to the north, the birth of the northern lights started its display. With greater and greater intensity, the blue-green lights eventually shot across the entire sky.

"Look, Silvia, the northern lights! I have seen pictures of them in magazines but never in real life. These are so vivid! The beautiful darkness of this sky over the ocean makes a perfect backdrop! This is just wonderful!"

As they continued to view God's fireworks from their balcony, the shape of the delightful glow evolved into what looked like curtains waving all around their inn and soaring up into space forever. God's spectacle lasted another twenty minutes, and as soon as it appeared, it then faded away. Another display of northern lights would surely come back again to delight those who take the time to look up into God's sky.

&

The rest of Adam and Silvia's short vacation went by like a few flickers of a candle. Before they knew it, they were packing up again and walking to the car, with their two suitcases in tow. Silvia stopped for a minute and turned around.

"What's the matter, Silvia? Did you forget something?"

"No, I didn't forget anything, and I do not want to forget this place. Give me a minute to look at our lovely inn one more time before leaving."

With the silence speaking to them both, they just stood on the red-brick walkway, looking at their surroundings. Then it was time to repack the car and head for home. Once on their way, Silvia took out the road map again just to make sure they didn't make a wrong turn somewhere.

Sometimes a memory would jump into Adam's mind when driving or riding in a car for a while. As they drove along twists and turns with rocky ocean views, Adam was entertaining one of those memories, which he decided to share.

"Say, Silvia, I wanted to tell you what happened to me about a month ago while on my evening walk. I think I may have offended our neighbors down at the next corner."

Now with her own thoughts broken, Silvia turned to Adam and said:

"You mean the sweet couple, Dale and Deloris? You may have offended them?"

"Yes, they are the very ones. Let me tell you how it happened."

Silvia breathed out a feminine sigh and said, "I am not sure I want to know. Well, maybe. Oh, Adam, go for it. Tell us all, the whole world is waiting."

Adam slowed down for a stop sign and then continued with his account.

"So…since it was after 8:00 p.m and getting darker during my walk, I could not see all that clearly. At any rate, while I continued to walk, I came across a skunk just about ten feet, maybe a little less from me! Yes, Silvia, a real live skunk! He was minding his own business next to the light pole, but I surely did not want to frighten him. Well, what do you know? Our neighbors were standing near the light pole too. Yes! Dale and Deloris were even closer to the skunk than I was…maybe two feet! The odd thing was that they did not even appear to know the darn skunk was there at all!"

Silvia commented, "Oh my, oh my, Adam, what in the world did you do?"

Adam continued with his story after carefully looking for any traffic at the upcoming intersection. He looked both ways, then slowly stepped on the accelerator pedal and finished his story.

"I am glad you asked what I did, Silvia. Now thinking fast on my feet as you know I always do…"

Silvia had to snicker a little about that self-assessment but remained silent and respectfully attentive.

"I carefully joined the couple and, as softly as possible, explained that a mere two feet away from their feet was an old, ugly skunk. Well, they looked at me, then directly at the skunk, and said:

"Adam, that is not a skunk—that is our new puppy dog!"

After hearing this, Silvia just about climbed clear through the car's windshield.

"Adam, I hope you apologized! Please tell me you apologized!"

CHAPTER

14

Getting Back to Business

Walt was taking care of some customers in the market when his parents came in through the back door of the loading dock. When he saw them, Walt excused himself from the lady who was asking how to tell if a cantaloupe was ripe for eating.

"Mom, Dad, it is so good to see you. I am really tired!"

Without wasting any time, Adam took his store apron down from the metal coat hook in the wall and started checking over the produce meanwhile Silvia went upstairs to take both luggage cases back to their apartment. While discarding older fruit into the galvanized metal waste basket, Adam said:

> "We had a great time, Walt, but we did miss
> you too. At dinner tonight, let's talk about the
> Tinker boys."

Six hours later, the Walkers gathered upstairs for a simple dinner. Silvia made a fresh salad from the market's produce while pan-frying some chicken, which later she would cut up and put on top of the salad. For a dressing, she made an Italian mix using olive oil, vinegar, and herbs from her kitchen. After placing the salad in the center of the table, Adam gave thanks in prayer.

"Dear heavenly Father, we have so many things to be thankful for. Please accept our praise and thanks for our countless blessings. As you continually keep us in your grace, also please help Zinc Bitter. He needs your help in ways that only you must know, so please be with him as he deals with his hardships. Also, graciously bless Francis and her father, Abe. Help them cope with the loss of Abe's wife… little Francis's mom. In Jesus's name, we pray. Amen."

After the prayer, Walt reached for some salad and said:

"You prayed for Zinc, the boy from church. He also goes to my school. Gosh, he is so withdrawn. During lunch, he never eats…says something like he is on a diet or that he is allergic to school cafeteria food. He never talks to anyone. I don't think he has any friends, but one day, Nancy, from my class, gave him twenty-five cents to buy a school lunch. He ate the whole lunch in five minutes flat."

While the salad and the dressing were being passed around, Silvia added that either she or Adam will try to converse with Zinc one Sunday after church.

"So, Mom and Dad, I talked with the Tinker boys' parents. They thought it would be a good idea for them to make short deliveries. Their dad could drive them to our market on his way to work. They have a pickup truck and can put their bicycles in the truck bed. In the late afternoon, their mom said she will drive them back home in their second pickup.

"I can still use my bike to make Lady Remington's deliveries. Oh, another thing, I almost forgot. You know how our Philco television has not been working right? Well, I took the tubes out from the back of the set and checked them with our tube tester. Guess what? I found two worn-out ones. I replaced those two tubes with new ones. It was a snap, and our black-and-white television works just fine now."

Adam had a smile on his face as big as when he and Silvia were on the Ferris wheel.

80

Two days later, George and Carmen Tinker gathered their boys, Thomas and Sherman, together in their kitchen. Mrs. Tinker poured milk and had chocolate cookies on a china plate for them. While the boys munched their cookies, the father spoke for both himself and their mom:

"Well, boys, how is your summer going?"

Both boys answered in unison, "Swell, Dad, why do you ask?"

"I was wondering if you would like to make some money at Walker's Market on Thursdays, if you are not too busy."

Jumping up from his seat at the kitchen table, Thomas was first to answer his dad:

"Yes! Yes! Yes! What will we do?"

Mrs. Tinker took it from there and spelled out the details. Walking to the broom closet located just off the kitchen, she retrieved a brown bag that was from Barton's Hardware Store.

"Now, Thomas and Sherman, we have faith that you two gentlemen will do what you are told…and do a good job for the Walkers. Right?"

Again, in unison, both boys agreed. So with that assurance, Carmen Tinker took out two shiny new metal baskets from the brown paper shopping bag.

"These are to mount on the front of each of your bikes. You will need them for the market food deliveries."

The boys were beside themselves. Presenting the baskets to her boys' outstretched hands, she added:

"Maybe this job will keep both of you rascals out of Mrs. Remington's coal bin."

Thomas and Sherman looked at each other with wide-eyed amazement. How in the world did their mom know about playing *king on the mountain* on the coal pile in the cellar?

CHAPTER
15

Another Community Meeting

Days marched on in Port James as villagers went among their business. For the most part, life was secure and quiet. There was almost no need for a police department or foot patrols, but it felt good to know the sheriff by his first name as he walked through the town. Sheriff Jake made it a point to pop his head into each business from South Avenue to Orchard Avenue as he made his rounds.

While walking on his route one morning, Jake checked his wallet, then his pockets, and found he had enough change to buy a blueberry turnover made from Maine's famous blueberries. After leaving Barton's Hardware on Fourth Street, his next stop was Beth's Bakery on the corner of Maple Avenue.

Beth was quite talented with her baking abilities, and all her pastries proved it. Her shop's display cabinet was in the shape of a horseshoe. As customers entered the bakery, a sweet aroma of either icing or pastry breads or both gently greeted them. Glass cabinets filled with pies, colorful cupcakes, and turnovers were pleasantly arranged in the center. On the left side, the glass cabinets held a whole assortment of tasty Italian cookies. To the right were examples of wedding cakes and cakes for any other occasion. These looked so real but were just for ideas and display.

Sheriff Jake entered Beth's Bakery with his pocket change in his hand. Beth was at the counter with Nichole, her daughter. They were checking their inventory of baking supplies and looked up when Sheriff Jake walked in. With a warm smile, Beth greeted him:

> "Good morning, Jake! How's it going today?
> Do you want your normal treat?"

Jake placed his change on the counter and said:

> "You bet, Beth. It's not a morning without your blueberry turnover! Say, Nichole, how is your boyfriend, Patrick? If you two ever get married, he would be one lucky man. You are as pretty as your mom and talented in the bakery department as well!"

Nichole turned two shades of red as she said that Patrick still makes her head spin. Taken back a little by her truthfulness and her boldness, Jake replied:

> "Well, now I better get going. You ladies have a great day!"

With a little blueberry stain left on his lips, Sheriff Jake continued his foot patrol toward Walker's. As he entered the market, he saw Walt at the cash register and his parents toward the back of the store. Picking up an apple to examine it, Jake placed it back on Adam's white wooden fruit stand, which had not yet been wheeled outside for the morning. Jake said to the Walkers:

> "Top of the morning to you all! Silvia, how was your trip last week? Walt was running his legs off while you were gone. You have a good kid here."

From the middle of the market, Silvia walked up to Jake while wiping her hands on her apron.

"Thanks for the complement about Walt. Yes, he takes after his dad…one great and hardworking guy. Oh yes, our trip was just fabulous! Our inn was so quaint, and the breakfasts were wholesome—they really stayed with you. Have you ever heard of Marginal Way? It is a mile-long footpath along one of our God's best creations. Perkins Cove was just charming with little boats, shops, and restaurants. You will have to go there sometime and take your family, or maybe just the two of you."

By this time, Adam came around from the third isle and greeted Jake with a handshake and said, "Besides all that, we attended a heifer judging!"

A little surprised, Jake was taken aback and said, "Hmm… this is the first time I ever heard about a heifer judging. Anyhow, it sounds like you had a great time. By the way, tonight is the village's community meeting at Kathy Reed's on the corner of Oak Avenue and Second Street. She wanted me to remind everyone I met on my rounds through the town. For some reason, this month's meeting will be at her home. So please don't forget to attend. As usual, it will start at six thirty. I'll see you folks tonight, okay?"

With that, Jake picked up an apple, and from his pocket, he placed a dime on the counter. Shining his apple on his shirt, he then turned around and left the market to continue his walk in the direction of the lighthouse.

For the Walkers, their day went rather quickly as there was a steady stream of customers. At five thirty, Silvia stopped long enough to go upstairs to retrieve a pot of homemade soup from the refrigerator and place it on the stove on the low setting. Coming back downstairs into the market, Silvia saw Adam wheeling his fruit and vegetable cart from the sidewalk outside.

"Say, Adam, let me get the door for you. We have to close up early for the community meeting at six thirty. Let's finish up in a few minutes. I have some vegetable beef soup on the stove for dinner."

With that announcement, Walt closed the entrance door facing the street and pulled the window shade down. On the shade was printed with words that read, "Closed. See you tomorrow." Walt and Adam followed Silvia upstairs. As they entered their apartment, the boys could smell the rich soup, one of Walt's favorite. Adam walked around the pool table to the bay window and opened it just a few inches to let in some outside breeze.

The air was warm and balmy, the kind of weather that made nearly all villagers felt blessed to be alive. Unfortunately, the only exception was poor Zinc. It was another night for him to be afraid at home. He knew just what to expect when his father came in the door. After working at the shipping docks, his father would have downed a few in the tavern just outside of town and was probably already mad at the world.

℘

That same evening, just as Jake said, Kathy offered her large living room for the community meeting. The back room of the library in town, where the residents usually met was being painted and would not be available.

Kathy had borrowed a few dozen folding chairs from the First Congregational Church and, with some help from the church elders, brought them over to set them up. Her living room was so spacious everyone could sit comfortably while attentive to Kathy in front of the group. Using one of her pedestal plant stands as a podium, Kathy placed her notebook in front of her. For a few minutes, she shuffled through her papers before starting the meeting. A few of the residents who had never visited her home before were whispering to each other about the room's beauty.

"Welcome, everyone, to my home, and thank you for coming to tonight's meeting. Most of you know I am Kathy Reed and will conduct the addenda of topics. Tonight, we have three items. We will have to consider each one separately, entertain any discussion, then take a vote if necessary. After these, I also have a topic of interest.

"For those who would like to stay a while after tonight's meeting, I have prepared some tea, coffee, and an assortment of Italian cookies from Beth's Bakery. We all know how delicious they are! So without further delay, I will get things started."

Kathy became a little uneasy, and from those attending, it was quickly apparent. At her makeshift podium, Kathy shuffled her white lined notebook papers a few more times, then briefly looked out her bay window before continuing:

> "Okay, please understand that several residents have brought this very same thing to my attention, so I agreed that I would put this on the addenda. I will need to address this to Mark Jones. Hello there, Mark. Thanks for coming tonight."

Everyone in the room moved several times to the right and left in their chairs in order to see where he was sitting. Mark, a middle-aged gentleman, was seated in the last of the three rows of chairs. Kathy continued:

> "It seems from several accounts that there has been some car traffic congestion near your house on West Road. In fact, Mark, there has been some near auto collisions. What I mean by that is several drivers have been distracted and bumped into each other. One mishap involved a car and the milkman's delivery truck."

Upon hearing this, Terry, the milkman, wiggled nervously in his chair and said:

> "That wasn't my fault! Waiting for the traffic light to change, my truck was completely stopped. I was in front of the Jones's house, and someone bumped into me from behind."

In order to keep anything from escalating unnecessarily, Kathy responded quickly:

> "I am not going to dispute whose fault it was with this or any other of the several auto mishaps on West Road. I am just stating the fact

that there is a distraction in Mark's front yard. Now, Mark, you must know that everyone has the most respect for your two twin daughters. They are great examples of how you and your lovely wife, Margret, have succeeded in raising your children. Let's see, if I remember correctly, they will be attending their fourth year of college next September...how time flies.

"Now all this traffic congestion and fender benders have come about from your daughters sunbathing on the lawn wearing the newest style of very small two-piece bikinis. For the sake of maintaining good traffic flow, could you ask them to sunbath in the backyard? I certainly hope your girls will not take offense to this. It surely is not meant that way."

Mark wanted this item to be over quickly, and quite frankly, he didn't even know his two daughters were doing this in the front yard. His face became a little red, and with his fingers, he was trying to pull his shirt collar away from his neck. Before a few more seconds were ticked off the clock, Mark composed himself and said:

"Oh sure, I will certainly tell them. You know, in their defense, it is nothing more than what you see at the beach these days. In fact, I don't understand these things like bikinis and rock and roll, but for the sake of safety, I will make sure they will use the backyard. Oh...uh... thanks for letting me know about this."

Silvia and Adam looked at each other, shared a little smile, but kept quiet. Some of the men in the room thought this was the best opening of a community meeting they ever attended. However, without any exception, all the fathers with teenage girls made a mental note to talk to their daughters about exclusively using their backyard for sunbathing activities. Feeling pleased that this issue went rather smoothly, Kathy continued with the next item on the addenda:

> "Very good, and thank you, Mark. Now item number two: George and Carmen Tinker would like to open a country restaurant, three miles south on West Road, near where they live. They rent a section of Lady Remington's mansion, and the old inn they want to renovate for a restaurant is just a mile farther south just as you leave town...if that means anything to anyone. Now they understand that their request will have to be presented to the zoning board for approval. They just wanted to know if anyone attending tonight would be opposed to their plan. They cannot be here this evening, but they tell me that they intend to restore and upgrade that old, abandoned inn by themselves. They are going to call it *Tinker's Country Kitchen*. I believe there is a barn on the same property, which I think is just around back. So would anyone have any opposition if their endeavor goes through?"

Looking over her bifocals at the group in her living room, Kathy waited a minute. Since she did not hear any negative comment, she continued on to the next evening's item.

"This is a biggie, folks. As you all know, about this time of year, the planning committee for *Christmas at the Shore* meets to begin organizing this yearly winter event. Our wonderful festival located at Gray Cliff lighthouse had been an attraction for many out-of-town families and also for Port James residents.

"In the past, we have had Santa and Mrs. Clause for the children. It is so adorable to see little ones sit on Santa's lap and tell what they want for Christmas presents. As you also know, we always have a live nativity scene located on the hill just before the lighthouse area. The nativity scene is complete with a real donkey, two real sheep,

Mary and Joseph, the wise men, and one shepherd. A few years back, we even had a live baby in the crib. Oh yes, in the lighthouse gift store, there are always some venders selling roasted chestnuts, hot chocolate, and coffee. I always look forward to the delicious aroma and the beautiful golden glow of candlelights that flow from those open windows.

"Every Christmas season, I love to watch the little children in their snowsuits stepping up onto the horse-drawn hayrides. They always wave, laugh like crazy, and sing carols as the horses pull the wagon through the paths around the lighthouse. Gray Cliff lighthouse is always decorated with a spiral of garland starting from the ground and going clear up to the very top. A few times, we even had some Charles Dickinson's characters from *A Christmas Carol* walking our streets."

At that point in Kathy's review of *Christmas at the Shore*, she stopped abruptly and looked at her neighbors in complete silence. Taking off her glasses, tears filled her eyes as she looked from left to right without really focusing on anything in particular. Everyone instantly felt the uneasiness of not knowing what was to come next. Sheriff Jake took a linen hanky from his pocket and offered it to Kathy, then sat back down again. Kathy dabbed her eyes and composed herself enough to continue.

"Well, my friends, it seems like we will never be able to have this festival again at the lighthouse or in Port James...and I mean *never*. See, now that we are living in the 1950s, there is this thing called *The Separation of Church and State*. Last evening while I was sipping tea on the front porch, a man drove up and introduced himself as 'Mr. Taxpayer.' He would not give me his real name, just 'Mr. Taxpayer.'

As you probably all know, I own the antique store on Maple Avenue and Third. I recognized him as the same man who stands under our canvas awning at my store to get out of the rain. He waits for the crosstown bus nearly every day but never comes into my store to buy anything. Because of what he said last evening at my house, I jotted down his car license plate as he drove off. I needed to know if he was a resident of Port James. Sheriff Jake was kind enough to check his files at the office and found that this man is a resident who lives at the far side of town.

"Good people…my dear friends and neighbors, here is the bottom line. Residence's tax dollars cannot subsidize this religious festival. We will no longer be able to use village electricity, village police, the village grandstand for Santa, or the village road crew guys for cleanup."

At this time, Kathy apologized for tearing up and said she needed to compose herself a little since this is so emotional for her. Without saying more, she left the room to get a drink of cold water in her kitchen. The room was still, and everyone in the group just sat there, completely stunned. A few minutes later, Kathy came back into the room and walked up front to her makeshift podium. Through the partly open front bay windows, the Catholic Church's steeple bells several blocks away could just be heard chiming the hymn "A Mighty Fortress Is Our God." A few people looked out the window in silence. Sheriff Jake raised his hand to speak.

Kathy saw Jake's hand in the air and said, "Jake, you don't have to raise your hand to talk. Anyway, do you have something to add?"

Now in the assessment of many people there that night, God entered into the hearts of his people in a wonderful and delightful way. Jake, feeling the spirit of God in him, offered this:

> "Kathy, if it would help at all, I will volunteer my time as sheriff for this festival."

Then, one by one, like the soft roll of the ocean in a peaceful and still evening, villagers freely offered their time and talents. George from Port James road crew volunteered for cleanup. Farmer Frank volunteered his horses to pull the wagon along the lighthouse paths. The Walkers offered to donate any electrical costs that would be incurred. Carpenter Larry said he would gladly build a removable stage. Thirty-three other residents generously offered their time to help keep the festival alive. Kathy passed around a clipboard and pen for everyone to write their names and telephone numbers on the list that grew and grew.

Beth from Beth's Bakery encouraged five others to be a team of bell ringers to solicit donations. Pulling their chairs together, they were already assigning various street corners for each to ring their bells. Money collected would surely cover any incidental costs.

In this way, some say God knew how this festival was to be saved.

With the villagers feeling their hearts glowing, Kathy and everyone present shared smiles, handshakes, and pats on the back with each other. Looking on from the podium, she was so proud of her villagers. She certainly did not want to shorten this perfect moment, so she waited a while before continuing.

"Everyone, thank you so much for what will certainly be the most meaningful *Christmas at the Shore* festival! Now lastly, I have this announcement of interest. I am sure Farmer Frank will not mind me announcing this to you all. Is that right, Frank?"

Taking off his gold wire-rimmed eyeglasses and cleaning them with his hanky, Frank gave a little grin and said:

"Oh sure, I don't mind at all. Go right ahead. Who knows, some people might find it interesting."

"Well… Frank has ordered sixteen boxes of live baby chickens for his new chicken coop at his farm, located over there on Valley Road. The chickens are expected to arrive at the post office here in the village on Oak Avenue tomorrow. So if you are mailing anything at the post office tomorrow morning, you might hear some cheeping. If you do, now you will know what in the world *that* is all about.

"Unless there is any more new business, that was the last item to bring up. Again, thank you all for coming this evening. If some of the men could fold up the metal chairs and stack them next to the door, it would be a great help. Now let's go into my dining room for refreshments."

CHAPTER

16

Chicken Talk and a Cry for Help

Having its share of retirees along with working families, Port James enjoys the mix of people in different stages of life, making for a diversified and interesting village population. The working men and women bring money into the village by shopping locally, somewhat more than the retired folks. On the other hand, the older generations have time to participate with volunteering their time around town. They help with the annual spring cleanup of litter, donating time at the Gray Cliff lighthouse, performing light routine tasks at their various churches and other similar work.

However, with a little more available time, some events such as the mail delivery of chickens became the prime talk of the retirees. After the community meeting held at Kathy's, Sally, Bertha, Janet, and Olivia got on their kitchen wall phones at home. They couldn't wait to be the first to announce to their closest friends about the next day's arrival of the chicks. After the first people were called, they immediately called several other retired friends who would not want to miss this once in a lifetime event.

So it was at the post office the next morning that Deloris Timely, the post office clerk, saw an astonishing sight through her lobby front window. A few blocks away was an assemblage of retired women and men heading her way. The women had their hair pulled back in buns, and most of the men wore baggy pants pulled up to their chests. It appeared that they were walking toward her like an overly excited friendly invasion.

Once arriving inside, the happy and excited mass of spectators woke up the chicks that were sleeping in every one of the sixteen boxes. One hundred and forty-eight chicks responded to the noise, the waving hands, and the general commotion with a chorus of their own tweeting. It was a hubbub not to be missed. In this small post office lobby, Deloris could not distinguish between the noise of the villagers and the chicks tweeting excitingly. However, from above all the commotion, she did hear things from the group like the following:

"Aren't they the cutest things you ever seen?"

"Do they have enough to eat and drink in those boxes?"

"Chicks mailed in a box! What will they think of next?"

"Grandma, can I have one to take home?"

Deloris was not used to such a spectacle in her post office, and as much fun as it was, she could not think of how to control this enthusiastic mass of villagers. As fate would have it, she did not have to find a way. From Oak Avenue out front, a woman's helpless scream pierced through the open door.

Everyone took their attention from the arrival of the chicks to Lady Remington who was outside pointing down to the storm sewer grate near the sidewalk. In no time at all, the post office became empty and was replaced by a circle of people outside with Lady Remington in the center. Poor Lady Remington was shaking and crying. Sheriff Jake gently pushed through the crowd to the uncontrollable, quivering woman. Lady Remington, who was upset to the point of hysterics, cried out,

> "Oh my God…look, Sheriff! That little chipmunk has wedged himself in the sewer grate. He can't move either way, and I am afraid he will die! Can you do something for him, maybe CPR, or some other first aid? Just a moment ago, he was free, and now he is locked up and almost dead! This little one surely did not want this to happen, nor did he ever deserve this."

Jake knew very well that Lady Remington was talking about the trapped animal, only he was privy to even more horrible knowledge about Lady Remington. She was reliving her own life's experience. At one time, not so long ago, she too was trapped like this little one. Not because of anything she had done wrong. Years ago, this poor, fragile lady had experienced total helplessness. During that time of her life, she wanted to be out of her body, and somehow, she also wanted to escape her own mind. For her, both awful feelings were a jail to her soul, which she could not live with. Lady knew only death could possibly free her.

Sherriff Jake kneeled down next to the rodent. With the strength of a giant, but with the gentleness God gave him, he carefully lifted the chipmunk and placed him in his linen handkerchief. Looking into Lady Remington's tear-filled blue eyes, mascara flowing down her rouge-painted cheeks, he softly spoke to her:

> "I'm truly sorry for this loss of God's little creatures. The little fellow deserved to live this summer. I will promise you, Mrs. Remington, that I will give him a fitting and proper funeral."

Lady Remington straightened her black pleated dress, readjusted her dark nylon stockings, then took a large breath to compose herself. By this time, Jake was moving the crowd away from Lady. She waited at the grate until he came back to her. Jake's understanding tones in his voice had reassured her for a while. After she nodded yes to Jake's comforting words a few times, she looked back one more time at the grate. Lady Remington then mounted her bicycle and headed home, saying the Lord's prayer to herself.

A Lesson in Being Quiet

It was Sunday again, and Silvia showered with Alfonso's singing from another opera aria through the shower wall. Considering everything, she thought to herself that it was a pleasant way to start her day. She would rethink this, of course, when, Alfonso's wife, Maria, moved back into town and took *her* morning showers. If the Walkers' morning shower schedule stayed the same, Adam would be showering while Maria sang selections from the Madam Butterfly opera.

This was one of those few days that Maine's weather pattern delivered warm morning temperatures. To help circulate the air in the sanctuary, ten minutes before the church service, the ushers cracked open the narrow windows on each side. The cooler ocean breezes were a welcome gift to the worshippers, especially for the choir members up front. The choir wore full-length polyester robes, the fabric of which was just invented in 1951. They looked good but were hot. At the appropriate time in the service, the choir sang the Sunday's anthem, directed by the church organist. For the anthem, he was standing upfront next to Pastor Westman and facing the choir.

The organist was very pleased that George and Carmen Tinker had joined the choir even though they were so busy with plans of opening a restaurant. With the Tinkers in choir these past months, it was the first time he had a full complement of all four sections—sopranos, altos, tenors, and basses.

Throughout the service, and every so often, George and Carmen would look down from the choir's location toward the congregation to make sure their boys were behaving themselves. This morning, both Thomas and Sherman were whispering to each other about the money they made delivering groceries with their bikes for Walker's. Sitting near the boys, Adam and Silvia noticed the youngsters were certainly acting fine but were gradually becoming louder with their discussion. Disapproving glances were directed to the brothers from each parent up front in the choir but were useless in quieting them. Eventually, both boys were pestering each other with poking and arguing.

Seeing and hearing what was happening, Adam motioned to Silvia, and they both slid over to the boys who were in the same church pew as them. Walt wasn't sitting with his folks since he was the acolyte for this Sunday's service. He was sitting upfront, next to the pastor, the choir, and the choir director. As soon as Adam and Silvia slid over, Thomas and Sherman settled down, but then their "little boy" fidgets started again. Adam thought for a minute, rubbing his chin with his thumb and finger. He then gave each boy a blank page from the church bulletin and two sharp pencils that he just happened to have from his pocket. Outside of anyone else's ears, he bent down toward the boys and whispered something to both of them.

At this time during the service, Pastor Westman walked to the pulpit, turned on the little reading light, and started his sermon on faith. Silvia smiled at both boys, who were now obviously intent on the pastor's message. In fact, the boys were taking detailed notes with their paper and pencil. Apparently, they were recording everything the pastor said. After the service was over, Silvia said to Adam:

"You truly impress me, darling. How you settled down the boys was a real blessing. I just don't know how you got them to concentrate so much on the pastor's sermon. I can't wait to see the notes they took during Pastor Westman's message."

By this time, they were waiting in line to shake Pastor's hand. Silvia moved ahead of Adam, bent down a little, and said to both boys:

"Can I see what you did in church today?
You were so quiet but working so hard listening
to the pastor's sermon!"

Thomas was more than happy to show his work and handed his paper to Silvia. Sherman took his page and placed it on top of Thomas's page so that Silvia would see his first. She first looked at both pages with a smile that turned into a questionable look of incomprehension. Silvia saw illustrations of arrows, dotted lines, arches, and stick figures. Handing them back to both boys who each were prouder than a Georgia peach, she turned back around and looked at Adam for a reasonable explanation.

"What was all that about, Adam? I didn't understand a single thing from their notes about Pastor's sermon."

Adam was hoping that it was time to shake Pastor Westman's hand so that Silvia's question would be sidelined and forgotten. Unfortunately, totally slowing down the line, a lady in front of them was bending Pastor's ear about some rosebushes. With this extra time, Silvia once again looked at Adam for his answer. Adam pretended to cough a little to buy some time, but Silvia didn't fall for that tactic.

"Adam, come clean with this and be honest. Don't forget, dear, you are in church and just had Holy Communion. Well?"

Adam knew he wouldn't win this one, so he tried to present his response in a way to make him look good.

"Well, Silvia, I know you think I have mysterious powers, and that certainly is true. To keep the boys quiet, all I told them was to draw how they would climb up the church walls jumping here and there to reach the ceiling fans."

"Oh, Adam, we are almost ready to shake Pastor's hand. Don't tell him what they did during his fine message!"

Looking at the boys ahead of him, Adam answered, "Silvia, honey, I don't think that will be necessary. They are already telling the pastor as we speak."

Silvia just rolled her pretty blue eyes and gave a sigh. She then said, "Adam, I need another vacation… I think I am losing it."

CHAPTER

18

Our Father's Creating Hands

After shaking the pastor's hand and complimenting him on such a fine sermon, Adam made his way to the coffee-and-goodie table. He poured a cup of coffee for himself and found an oatmeal raisin cookie, a little larger than the others. With his coffee cup in one hand and the cookie in the other, he turned around and saw some of the youth of the church.

Several of the high schoolgirls and schoolboys were discussing the topic of world creation by science. In an increasing number of schools, this and evolution was starting to be taught as standard truth in the classrooms. When they saw Adam munching on his cookie, they asked him to join in on their discussion. Adam took it as a compliment that they asked him for what he thought about creation by science or creation by God. Sipping his coffee, he went over to the far end of the fellowship room with the teenagers following in a cluster. Walt was among the group and wondered how his dad would address these topics.

While the teenagers continued to talk with themselves, Adam went to the church supply closet and found enough small brown paper bags for each young adult. He gathered some dirt from an old flowerpot that was ready to be discarded and added a spoonful to each bag. When passing out the bags of dirt to each, he said to the group:

"Now, gentlemen and ladies, pretend that
your bag is the beginning of all creation."

119

Adam took his pocket watch from his vest. "See this beautiful pocket watch? Look inside, see all the wonderful workings, the springs, gears, and ratchets? Everything is put together just perfectly to tell time. Now shake your bags of dirt."

For two or three minutes, every child energetically shook their bags of dirt. Adam looked around at the group, all shaking their bags. He then said:

> "Look inside. Have you made a pocket watch? No? Then shake some more."

The teens shook and shook their bags, each making a rattling sound. With coffee cups in hand, some of the adults nearby were wondering what in the world their kids were doing. A few gathered near the collection of bag shakers to look on. After a few more minutes, Adam said:

> "Okay, you may stop and open your bags. Have you made a beautiful pocket watch? No, of course not. You could shake your bag forever and *never* make a watch. Now look at your own hand. It is so more perfectly made than a mere watch.
>
> "If shaking your bag of dirt forever could not make a watch, then certainly your bag of dirt could never make a living and growing hand like yours. No, it would be even more impossible that something living could come from your bag. Remember too, I gave you each a head-start by giving you some dirt. Before creation, there wasn't even dirt, only empty space."

Adam then went on to say: "As beautiful as the watch is, it is not alive and could *never* be alive. My young friends, your hand is so much more complex and amazing than a mere watch. If there is a scratch on a watch, will it repair itself like your skin can? Absolutely not! Then how can anyone believe that *everything* we see came from some dirt? Unless, of course, *everything was made from dirt by God*.

"See, ladies and gentlemen, the more you learn about science, the more you are actually learning about God. God owns science. Why do I say this? I say that because He made science. He made all the laws of biology, chemistry, physics…everything…everything we can see and all the things we cannot see.

"*Science is God's invention*. Without God, science did not exist and still cannot exist. With God's invention of science, God made the world and everything in it.

"I have no problem believing the whole universe was created by science, or evolution, or the big bang theory or whatever your teachers today call it, because I know God invented those things. You see, He is God, and God made these things work."

With that said, both the adults and teenagers gave a full and gratifying loud applause.

Riding in the car on the way home from church, Walt seemed to be all smiles. Within a few minutes, from the back seat, he reached forward to Adam's back and shoulder, giving it a little approving rub and said, "Hey, Dad, you did it again! Thanks!"

CHAPTER
19

Safe at Home but Not for Everyone

Zinc walked home from church with the good pastor's message replaying in his mind. Pastor Westman paraphrased various psalms from the bible by saying:

> "Give your burdens and concerns to the Lord, and he will provide for your needs. The Lord's mercy and compassion is great from heaven. Do not be either dismayed or ashamed to wait for the Lord in your life."

The boy had made it home from church, just in time for his father to meet him on the concrete steps at the front of their house. Between slobbering fits, his father managed to say:

> "Hey, boy, how was that girly church? Did you find your way to heaven? Did you put in a good word for your old man?"

With those words said, his father grabbed Zinc's hair and pulled him up the outside stairs to the front door. With one push to his chest, Zinc went stumbling backwards through the unlatched door and onto the tile foyer.

"Now you are going to learn a good lesson from above! You will be seeing God real soon, boy!"

With a knee on poor Zinc's chest, his father delivered blow after merciless blow to his son's head way after his face broke into bloody, painful welts. Looking up between blows, Zinc could only see a blur of fists. His own blood mixed with his father's bleeding knuckles… bloody red from countless hits to the child.

Finally exhausted, his father got off Zinc and used his heel to kick his precious son across the room and into the far corner.

"What a worthless piece of garbage you are! You are all skin and bones, no muscles like me. I should have taken care of you when you were born…like I did with your mother. Why don't you just die and make it better for me!"

His father looked at his own bleeding knuckles. Grabbing an empty whiskey bottle from the kitchen counter, Marvin smashed it onto the floor, scattering broken glass pieces at his defenseless, whimpering child. With that departing gift, he turned away from Zinc and staggered down the dark hallway into his bedroom for a well-deserved nap.

∞

A few hours past, maybe more, Zinc could not make out what time of the day it was and, for that matter, even what day it was. The last he could remember was Sunday after church. He was still in the corner, all crippled up with dried blood on his poor, swollen face. It was still Sunday, and it was dinnertime, not that it mattered to Zinc. The poor boy hadn't had a decent dinner for months.

How can such torment exist only a few blocks away from a quiet, loving family? It's almost impossible to think of the extreme dichotomy of such things within the same village. Even so, the Walkers were ready to sit down to eat a nice Sunday turkey dinner, which both Adam and Walt were looking forward to all morning.

Silvia felt that a perfect turkey dinner with all the fixings should be made several times throughout the year, not just on Thanksgiving Day.

Silvia pulled the aluminum foil off the top of the turkey in the oven and set the dial to *broil*. She liked to do this for the last five or ten minutes to make the turkey skin beautifully brown and crispy in texture. Looking around her kitchen area, Silvia said to herself:

> "Let's see…mashed potatoes topped with melted butter, green beans, sweet potatoes with marshmallow topping, cranberry sauce and Mandurian orange slices mixed with walnuts. For dessert, homemade apple pie. Good! I did not forget anything."

Turning around to her boys who were watching a baseball game on the television, she cupped her hands around her mouth and announced:

> "Gentlemen, after washing up, help me get everything to the table, please."

Adam and Walt wasted no time. Both men jumped up and headed to the bathroom sink to wash hands. After soaping up, rinsing off, and towel drying—quicker than a mermaid's wink—they dashed into the kitchen area to help Silvia bring the serving platters of food to the table. With everything ready to eat, Silvia asked Walt to offer up a table prayer. Lowering their heads and closing their eyes, this fortunate family of three held hands with each other, ready to talk to God.

"Dear heavenly Father, you have graciously blessed us with this food we are about to partake from your harvest. We thank you for this bounty and ask that you use us for your work here on earth. Amen."

Before eyes were opened and heads raised, Silvia felt the Holy Spirit moving her to add to the prayer:

> "And dear Father, protector of your children, we ask that you look after Zinc Bitter. We do not know what is happening to this poor child of yours. We don't know what we can do to help him. You have given us Romans 8:26, which tells us that even if we do not know what we should pray for, the Holy Spirit will pray for us. So we are praying, Lord, and as Walt said, help us to help others, especially Zinc. Amen."

After these dinner prayers, Adam slid his chair away from the table and stood up. At the head of the table, Adam started the meal by carving the turkey. The white meat was juicy and tender, and the turkey skin was crispy and tasty with light seasonings. As other plates and bowls of food were getting passed around the table, Adam placed his carving knife and fork on the platter. Looking with love at Walt and Silvia, he added praise for God by saying to his family:

> "The Holy Spirit is real and, by God's promise, is living with us every moment of our lives. We stumble through life, making mistakes and every so often doing things right. It is a blessing that our Creator has left us with His Holy Spirit to help us every day."

Taking a Break

It had been much too long since Adam and Silvia had their three days away. So after dinner while Silvia started washing the evening dishes, they talked with Walt once again. He assured them he was perfectly fine with filling in at the market for a short time. With that arranged, Adam walked to the couch and started looking at the Rand McNally road map. Walt would normally ask his dad for a game or two of pool but decided to get to bed early. He recalled how exhausted he was from the last time he ran the market by himself. After those three days, even though he was in great shape, everything hurt on his body. He laughed to himself that even his hair hurt. Turning to his parents while putting on a light jacket, he said:

> "I am going for a quick walk around the block, then I think I will go to bed early. I'll probably shower after my walk instead of rushing around tomorrow morning."

The evening was cool with a slight breeze coming from the ocean. The streetlamps were just starting to illuminate, which helped Walt make out more details on the front porches that he walked past. He made a brisk pace going down Maple Avenue then left onto

West Road. Slowing down his gait, Walt turned the block on South Avenue going past Melvin Bitter's house. Out of the corner of his eye, he thought he saw someone moving from one room to the next. It looked like Zinc, but he was all bent over like an old man. Maybe it was his father Melvin, but the image looked too thin to be him.

Walt had one of those feelings that something was wrong in that house, but what? Did God want him to go up to the door and see if he could do anything? Walt continued to walk, but he still had the image in his mind of opening Melvin's door and looking inside. Each of his steps led him a little farther away, and after a minute, Walt was well past the house. Shaking the image from his mind, he thought to himself that at least he could pray for Zinc. Stopping next to the mailbox on the sidewalk, he placed his folded hands on the cool metal top and bowed his head to deliver a short but sincere prayer for Zinc. Walt paused one more time to look back at the house, which was now about a half block away. With a sigh, he walked up Third Street and headed back home.

When Walt arrived at the market, he walked around back then went up onto the loading dock. Stopping briefly to look for his key, he noticed the light to his parents' bedroom had just turned off. Gosh, he felt safe and secure and even more importantly *loved*. How he wished that everyone could feel this way, especially Zinc.

Once inside, Walt took a quick shower, dried off, and slipped on some pajamas. After getting between the sheets of his bed, he fell to sleep within a few moments.

The next morning, before his parents left for their outing, Walt found his dad in the bathroom whistling happily. While leaning against the doorway of the bathroom, Walt said:

> "Dad, as you have seen, the Tinker boys are doing great with their local grocery deliveries. I plan to have them work for more than just one day a week. It should work out fine as long as their parents can transport them and their bikes in the morning and then again in the evening."

In the bathroom, Adam was placing the finishing touches on his hair with his pocket comb. He looked in the mirror and noticed how Walt's facial reflection looked so much like his. Walt was truly becoming a man and taking on manly responsibilities. Turning around to face his son, Adam answered:

> "Sounds like a good idea. Keep in mind, however, that their parents are hoping to open a restaurant sometime rather soon. I am not so sure that they will have the time to transport the boys, but it certainly doesn't hurt to ask."

From the kitchen area, Silvia called Walt's name, "Hey, Walt? I will be packing a picnic lunch for your dad and my outing. What kind of sandwich would you like me to leave for you? I can make it and put it in the refrigerator."

Walt said to not worry about him and that he would probably put together some leftover turkey for himself. Adam left the bathroom and, when passing Walt in the hallway, gave him an approving nudge on his shoulder. Looking toward the kitchen area, he focused on Silvia who was at the counter near the sink. Still a few feet away, Adam said:

> "Silvia, my love, I was thinking of having lunch out at a restaurant today."

He then waltzed up to his wife and quickly twisted her around so that she was facing him. Quite surprised, Silvia slightly parted her moist lips as she looked into Adam's eyes for an answer to his action. Looking at her sweet, questioning face, with the tip of his finger, he gently outlined her lips, the side of her face, then her chin. Giving her a wink, he said:

> "Hey, little lady, take advantage of this *limited-time offer for lunch*. I am paying for both of us!"

With that announcement, Silvia winked back at him and returned the bread to the breadbox. She was surprised at herself that even for a beautiful, brief moment, Adam took her breath away. After that revelation, she straightened the kitchen counter so it would look nice when they returned for the evening. Turning once again to face her dear husband she said:

"Well, my handsome hunk, let's split this scene and take off like the wind!"

Hand in hand, they both went down the stairs from their apartment and into the market, which was still not open for the day. Walking through the aisles, Silvia spotted something she hadn't seen before. Stopping abruptly, she said, "What in tar nations is this machine?"

"Why, my beloved, you are now a proud owner of a fully electric coffee bean grinder! See, let me show you how it works. A customer makes their selection of coffee beans, then dials the size of grind they want. This machine can grind beans very fine for drip coffee or a little coarser for percolators. See, it's great! Our customers pour the beans into the top of this shoot, put the empty bag at the bottom, and then push the button. Within seconds, their beans are perfectly ground just the way they need."

"Adam… Adam… Adam…do you really think this will catch on? It surely sounds silly to me."

Adam anticipated Silvia's resistance, so quickly, he placed a handful of coffee beans in the shoot and turned on the grinder. Immediately, with a pleasant grinding noise, the fresh coffee grounds spilled into the bag. Acting like the salesman who sold him the machine, he waved his hand in a circle and toward her a few times so Silvia would catch the aroma of freshly grounded coffee beans.

"Oh my goodness gracious, Adam, *that certainly is a wonderful smell!* I could stay in this aisle all day sniffing this fantastic aroma, but you promised me a lobster lunch, so let's get going!"

Adam thought that showing Silvia the new coffee grinder went pretty well. He did make a promise to himself that *before* any future expenditures were made, it would include Silvia's agreement first. Silvia looked at Adam for a moment and said, "Adam, you are truly something else."

Walking to the market's front door, he pulled up its window shade and unlocked the latch, allowing Silvia to go in front of him. Once on the sidewalk, strolling side by side together, Silvia surprised her husband and gave him three light love-pats on his behind and said:

"Hey, Mr. Coffee Grinder Expert, how do you fancy my ponytail? I did that all for you, big guy!"

Adam knew this was going to be another great day with his Silvia. He was truly thankful to his creator for his life with his wife and son in Port James. While walking on Maple Avenue toward First

Street and Gray Cliff lighthouse, Silvia looked a little pensive then said:

> "Adam, I know I have mentioned this several times, but I've noticed that some residents of Port James don't travel far when taking vacations. Sometimes there is no need to. The natural surroundings all around Port James brings out-of-state families here to spend some of the nicest days of their vacations. So for today and our one day off, I am glad we decided not to waste travel time and instead just stay right where we live."

It was a short walk from the gas-lit village sidewalks to the sandy dirt pathway toward the Gray Cliff lighthouse at the top of the hill. God had delivered another beautiful morning. They were given a marvelous panorama view of rocky cliffs, white sandy beaches, and the gray-blue ocean. Behind them stood the lighthouse ever vigilantly scanning its horizon. To the right, Silvia noticed Lester, the lighthouse keeper, tending his small garden patch near the base of the stone structure. Walking over to him, Silvia touched his shoulder and said:

> "Hi there, Lester. Beautiful morning, isn't it?"

Lester rose to his feet and brushed off some fresh dirt from his knees. Once standing, he turned to her with a smile and replied:

> "Top of the morning to you both! Yes, I believe God made a good one today. Take a gander at that sailboat on the horizon, the one with the blue and white sail. I have been tracking it for some time now. I think it is headed to Portland for the sailboat races this afternoon. Are you two going up that way?"

Silvia looked at Adam for agreement, then back to Lester and replied:

>"Except for lunch, today we are going to enjoy your little paradise up here with the fresh air and scenery. Say, I really like what you are doing with those rosehip bushes and seagrass out there near the edge of the cliff."

Adjusting his straw hat a little, Lester thought for a moment, then said:

>"Yes, I planted the rosehips, but I had nothing to do with the seagrass. About ten years ago, the sandy part of this cliff was being eroded away to the ocean. It was occurring so quickly that we thought the lighthouse would eventually be washed away to the sea. I'm not sure if you know Lady Remington, but all by herself, she relocated thousands of seagrass plugs to where you see them now. I remember how she would pedal her old heavyweight bike with her side baskets filled with seagrass plugs. One by one, she made holes in the side of the cliff and carefully placed a plug into each hole.
>
>"Many engineers who have come to inspect said that ever since she did that, the erosion had slowed down more and more until after a few years it had completely ceased. See, she knew those plants rooting securely into the sand would keep the cliff from disappearing. She singlehandedly saved my lighthouse."

Adam was taking in the conversation but decided to mosey on over to the edge of the cliff. From his high vantage point, he viewed the early morning beach lovers walking down the path to the water and the narrow strip of sand. Nestled just past the rocky cliffs, visitors were finding places at the sandy cove for their beach umbrellas, blankets, and coolers. The sandpipers were doing their dance along the wet beach picking out sand shrimp for breakfast. High overhead, in the blue sky, a few seagulls were catching updrafts to soar without needing very much wing movement.

Adam wondered if the gulls were doing this for pleasure or to check out their next meal. In any case, this place was a delightful location for him and Silvia to relax and enjoy God's creation for the day.

Still conversing with Lester, Silvia bent down and picked a wild buttercup growing among the grass. Looking at its yellow glow in the sunshine, she said with some compassion in her voice:

> "Lester, I am glad you told me that account
> of Lady Remington. She goes to our church and,
> quite frankly, is rather mysterious. Our son Walt
> delivers her groceries once a month to her home.
> He knows to just knock on the door, then leave
> the paper bags of groceries on her front porch."

Lester looked at her for a minute and said, "Well, yes, but I think she is a good soul. There are some things about her that only a few villagers know."

Lester abruptly stopped his train of thought, measuring his words carefully, and said:

> "I can only speculate on things about that
> poor lady, and they may not be true. Say, do you
> want to climb to the top of the light? I'll wave to
> you when you get all the way up there!"

Silvia called to Adam who was now sitting on a rock near the cliff's edge. He was still looking out to sea taking it all in and was touching something in his pocket from time to time to make sure it was still there.

"Adam, honey, let's climb the lighthouse all the way to the top. Lester said we should...and there is not a cloud in the sky."

So with that, Adam joined Silvia. They walked over to the lighthouse and started the climb up the spiral staircase to the lamphouse at the top. As usual, Silvia was in the lead, but Adam didn't mind it a bit. Being two steps behind her on the spiral steps, he had a marvelous view of Silvia's pulsating, seductive leg muscles. Silvia paused halfway up to catch her breath, then called to Adam:

"How are you doing back there, Adam? Am
I going too fast for you to keep up?"

"Well, Ms. Legs, I can keep up just fine, and the view I have of you is just scrumptious, thank you!"

With that comment, Adam could almost envision Silvia rolling her pretty blue eyes, but she surprised him. Before taking another step, Silvia took her right hand and, in slow motion, provocatively rubbed her nice, firm calf muscle of her right leg up and down. In silence, she performed this a few lushes times, knowing quite well that she had Adam's fullest attention. Then in an instant, she gave an innocent laugh and increased her pace until she arrived at the top landing. Once there, she cupped her hands and whispered down to Adam, "Come and get me, Adam. I'm all yours!"

As soon as he caught up to her near the massive fourth-order Fresnel lighthouse lens, they ventured to the outside platform. Holding on to each other and the railing, they allowed the breezes to engulf them like a bath. Adam looked at his woman and said:

"Silvia, I love you. Thanks for being born."

"Oh, honey, I wondered if you may have forgotten that it is my birthday today!"

Adam took her hand and whispered, "Happy birthday, love. I hope you like this."

Adam reached into his pocket and handed her a small jewelry box. Inside was a silver pendant of a seagull with a delicate chain to wear around her neck. Adam almost never saw Silvia cry, except for the passing of his parents several years ago. Today, she was filled with tears.

"Oh, Adam, I love you so much! It's stunning! I will always wear it! Can you put it around my neck for me?"

Facing her, Adam took the pendant and reached around the back of her lovely smooth neck to clasp it together. She felt his warm, loving fingers on her skin, then with the softest of whispers in his ear, Silvia tenderly said:

"Adam, thank you for my present, and thank you for this day with me."

They remained on the outside landing, holding each other and taking in God's beautiful creation while sharing the warmth of their closeness. Silvia then placed both of her hands on Adam's shoulders and gave a playful push away. With a mix of laughter and giggles, she spun in circles, her new neckless swinging straight out as she turned. When she stopped twirling, Adam rushed over and caught her by the waist. The neckless found itself nestled quietly and perfectly in her cleavage.

"My oh my, Silvia, that silver seagull found a great place to land... Silvia, you are perfectly gorgeous. It's *you* that makes that pendant look beautiful!"

After almost an hour, they went back inside and descended the spiral staircase to the outside. Lester was done with his lunch and was shining the brass lighthouse plaque with a white paste cleaner and a soft cloth. He looked up from his work and said:

"Hi, folks! I grabbed a quick lunch in the lighthouse gift store, but just before I went inside, I waved to you when you were at the top...you didn't see me. Guess you were busy up there. Before starting on this plaque, I cleaned that park bench over there in the shade. It's all yours if you would like to sit for a while."

Adam took Silvia's hand, and together, they sat close to each other, like lovers. The light perfume from the rosehip gardens engulfed them on the white wooden bench. Breathing in deeply, they both took in the sweetness of the air around them. Adam gazed at the lighthouse, the birds in the sky, the faraway seagrass, then back to his lovely wife. Gosh, she was scintillating! Being this close together and in the sunlight, Adam noticed the sun was bringing out twelve or more cute freckles on and around his wife's cheeks and some on her cute nose. This time couldn't be more perfect, *she* couldn't be more perfect. Adam was in love with Silvia all over again.

By this time, they both noticed Lester walking over to the gift shop to check on things and to take a rest out of the sunshine. Adam waved his hand at Lester, catching his attention. Lester did an about turn and walked back over to them. Adam remarked:

> "Lester, thanks for all you do to keep this lighthouse and garden a place for so many to enjoy."

Lester looked at the couple and said, "You're welcome. I enjoy it, and every day, I feel that it is a privilege for me."

Lunch sounded good to Adam and Silvia, so they decided to make their way back into the village for a meal at the Port James Lobster Shack. The restaurant was just a short walk from Gray Cliff lighthouse. Outside its entrance is an oval wooden plaque displaying a red lobster. From the sidewalk, they could see white linen-covered tables with heavyweight silverware at each place setting. Every dinner plate sported a gray etching of a lobster in the center. Adam reached around Silvia to open the door for her.

Once inside, the waiter found them a table where they could look out the window and watch a sea lion resting on some wet rocks. Most of the tables in the restaurant were filled with customers, so they were thrilled with their table location and terrific view.

Silvia and Adam always enjoyed watching the sea life and promised to each other that one day soon, they should go on a whale watch on one of those boats that leave from Portland Harbor. After enjoying the meal, the view, and conversation, Silvia reminded Adam to make sure he left a nice tip for the waiter since he gave them the best table in the whole restaurant, not to mention bibs to wear while eating their lobster. Silvia was pleased that after such a wonderful but messy meal, neither of them had butter stains on their white cotton shirts.

After paying the tab, Adam nudged open the door for his woman. Feeling the sunshine on their faces, they headed down the sidewalk to the path and the sandy cove to enjoy the beach. Once on the footpath, Silvia noticed it was made of mostly coarse sand, so she took off her shoes and felt the warmth on her soft, bare feet; it was like a massage with each step.

They stayed at the cove until the incoming tide made the beach too narrow to remain any longer. With high tide at its peak, the ocean waves burst into a dancing spray onto the rocky cliffs. White foam mixed with saltwater finding its way into rock crevices and then quickly flowed back into the ocean for another play.

Looking at everything around them, with joy in her voice, Silvia exclaimed, "Adam, this is our Creator's playground! Maybe I'm wrong, but I can just imagine that He must have had so much fun making this area! And just think, He did all this with his own spoken words and his hands! Thank you, God!"

The path that took them down to the sandy cove was the same one they would take to get back up the hill. It had four or five turns, which made natural spots to rest and gaze out to sea. Adam and Silvia took advantage of each resting area. It gave them a nice view as they looked out to the ocean, enjoying the playful sprays of the water—such a wonderful spectacle. Silvia took Adam's hand feeling his warmth and love. She looked all around her and said:

> "Just think, every day when we are at work
> in our market about a half a mile away, all this is
> still happening at the shore! Every day, Adam! We
> are so busy with our lives that we don't even think
> about all this."

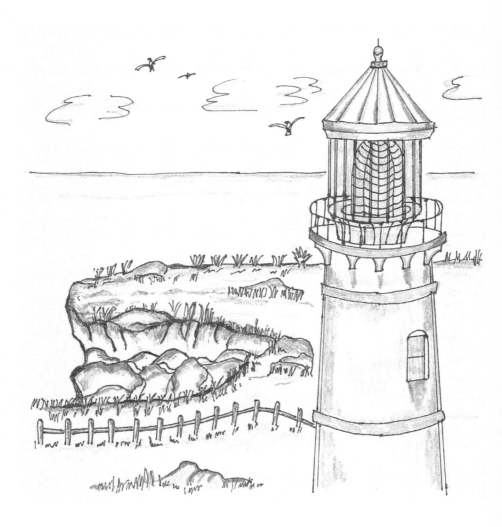

She took both of Adam's hands in hers and squeezed them tight.

"In the future, Adam, we need to take time to smell the rosehips and feel the salt spray on our faces and look at these magnificent views! After all, when you were courting me, this place was the setting for one of our earlier dates…remember that, Adam?"

CHAPTER

21

A New Business

It was only one week ago when the zoning board accepted their request to renovate the old inn for a restaurant. It was another thing, however, to acquire a business loan for their enterprise. George and Carmen Tinker got up early on the appointed day, donning their Sunday best clothes to meet with the official from the bank. The building was located on the corner of Fourth Street and Orchard Avenue.

Standing out on the sidewalk in front of the bank, they both took a deep breath and entered. Once inside, they waited in the seating area for the loan officer to greet them. With a measured smile and a token handshake, Mr. Curtis walked up and introduced himself with a professional tone in his voice. He then turned around and said for them to follow as he led the way to his office.

"Mr. and Mrs. Tinker, please have a seat. I have prepared the necessary paperwork for your commercial business loan." Looking at the collection of forms before them, George and Carmen felt swamped with all the paperwork. Right from the beginning, they thought that they might as well walk out and not waste the bank loan officer's time.

After only a few minutes, a teller knocked on his partially opened office door.

"Excuse me, Mr. Curtis, but could you help a customer in line 3? We need a signature from you."

Mr. Curtis gave a sigh and pushed his chair away from his desk and stood up while adjusting his tie. "So sorry, folks. This shouldn't take too long."

When he was well past earshot, Carmen said to George, "Did you hear what Mr. Curtis said? He called us 'folks.' Maybe he likes us and will give us the loan. What do you think, George? Do you think he likes us? George, are you not hearing me, or are you ignoring me? It's not nice to ignore your wife, George."

The first form asked them to sum up their own personal worth. Carmen looked at George who was just tapping his pen on the paper making a sound like a little parakeet crunching his seeds. With a little sigh, she said:

> "This portion shouldn't take too long. Although we have no outstanding bills or credit to declare, we also don't have any assists to speak of. Our two eight-year-old trucks are worth about four hundred dollars each, our furniture is nearly worthless…and that is just about it."

George was looking down, still feeling quite a little overwhelmed and personally dejected. Carmen reached over and cupped her hand under his chin, turning his face directly toward hers.

"George, look at me. What would be the worst thing that could happen? When we finish today, they just might decline us, and no harm would be done. So no matter how pointless it may seem to be for us, let's continue."

George thought what her reasoning made a lot of sense. By this time, Mr. Curtis came back and rearranged himself at his dark-wood swivel chair. The wheels squeaked lightly as he rocketed back and forth. Looking across his desk at the couple, Curtis seemed genuinely happy for them. Little did they know the bank was holding the title on the old, abandoned inn, and the board of directors wanted to have someone like the Tinkers purchase it and take it off the bank's hands. To acquire a loan, the Tinkers also had to fill in their business plan. That included the costs of everything that will be needed.

Besides the purchase of the inn and also the old barn out back, they had to include the cost of permits, insurances, renovation costs, staff salaries, and the purchase of food goods to stock the kitchen. There was a separate spot to include utility costs.

On yet another form, they had to write their projected gross and net revenues for the restaurant. It was just the best guess they could come up with. When this was all done, the loan officer Curtis said that the bank might just allow them to have a business loan of thirty years at 2.5 percent, payable on the first of each month. Basically, Carmen and George felt that they would be signing their lives away, and they were very nervous about it all.

Another question at the outset was the name of the new restaurant. They had toyed with a name but had not talked about it with each other very seriously. So right on the spot, Carmen wrote in the appropriate blank, *Tinker's Country Kitchen*. She said to George, "Well, we better stick to that name. It is now official."

After three full hours, Mr. Curtis collected all the papers, checking for any unintentional missing data. Looking mostly satisfied, he stood up and offered handshakes to them both while leading them to the door. With a smile, he said:

> "Give us six banking days, and I will call you with our decision. I will have to meet with the bank president and at least one board member. Have a nice day, Mr. and Mrs. Tinker, and thank you for thinking of us for your business bank loan."

Over the next five days, George and Carmen requested direction from God during their evening prayers. After one of those prayers, Carmen said to George:

> "No matter what the bank says about our loan, we must think of it as God's plan for us. So let's just be content either way."

On Friday Morning, Carmen and George were in their kitchen cleaning up after breakfast while Thomas and Sherman scampered off to the backyard to play tag. George was collecting the plates and silverware, stacking them next to the sink to be washed, while Carmen started filling up the sink with water and dish soap. She partly submerged her hand in the water and quickly swished it to make a collection of soap bubbles. When the wall phone rang, both knew it had to be Mr. Curtis from the bank with his news. Carmen look at George, then George looked at Carmen, then both looked at the phone. Carmen tried to decide if the ring sounded like it was delivering exciting or disappointing news for them.

After the fourth ring, Carmen said, "For heaven's sake, George, answer the phone! My hands are already wet with the dishes." Without any more hesitation, George ran over, picked up the receiver, and answered:

"Hello? Yes, this is George Tinker. Really? Are you sure? Well, I can hardly breathe...yes, sir, I agree, it is the right decision. Oh...and thank you for all your considerations and work, Mr. Curtis! Goodbye."

By this time, Carmen had dried her hands and impatiently stopped what she was doing to hear from George if they got the loan. Without any more waiting, she said:

"For crying out loud in a bucket, George, spill it! Did we get the loan? If we did, when can we pick up the check? Do we need to sign anything else? What should we wear to the bank? How late are they open today?"

George was just putting down the telephone receiver and hadn't said anything to Carmen. He didn't have the time to process any response to his wife's hundred questions. He just stood there in the kitchen with a half piece of buttered cinnamon toast still in his left hand.

Carmen was just about wild at this time. She took her wooden spoon from the center drawer and started chasing George around the kitchen, yelling:

"Tell me! Tell me! George, tell me! I love
you, but I'll break this darn spoon over your head
if you don't tell me right now!"

George knew he shouldn't push his luck any further, but he grabbed the other wooden spoon from the drawer and put it sideways in his mouth like it was a red rose. With his best ability, he started prancing around like a Spanish flamingo dancer, his hands waving over his head, snapping his fingers, and clicking his heels. Carmen started to laugh and, dropping her spoon on the floor, joined him. Together, they did a sort of a Conga dance line but looked more like two ducks who both drank from a large puddle of coffee. The rest of their morning would have gotten even wilder, but by this time, they wore themselves out and flopped on the couch. Carmen looked at George's smile and his red sweaty face and said, "I'm assuming we got the loan...and you better say yes!"

So now they were proud owners of their new business and also a proud owner of a thirty-year business loan. A few days later, they put their lives in the Lord's hands and gave their two-week notices at their work. Soon after, they were in full swing of their reconstruction work at the old inn.

⁊

Bright and early in the morning, out at the renovation site, their future restaurant hardly looked like a nice place to visit and eat, but that was to be expected. Inside the restaurant-to-be, George was on his tall aluminum stepladder, working on the ceiling. He descended the ladder, wiping his forehead with his back-pocket hanky. Once back on the floor, he looked around for their water thermos to take a cool drink. Carmen put her one hand on her hip and the other on her chin.

"George, the ceiling looks great. Will it match the floors? For these six windows at the front and side wall, what do you think of lacy white curtains to break up the dark wood? Do you think the curtains should have ties or keep them straight? How about the windowsills? Should we keep them natural wood or paint them white?"

After a quick swig of water, George answered, "For heaven's sake, Carmen, I can't keep up with all your questions!"

Carmen continued as if she didn't even hear George:

> "George, how about above the kitchen pass-through? Should we have antique lights, or should we install those modern florescent lights? The antique lighting would look nicer but may not be as efficient. I think the counters should be Formica. Hum…is the stain on the ceiling uneven, or will it look better when it is dry? I think it is because the stain is not dry…yes, I hope so anyway. What do you think? It's not wet is it?"

George interrupted Carmen's thinking and inserted, "Carmen, I have a great idea. I need to finish this ceiling, then work on the sink plumbing. Why don't you go to Barton's and pick out wallpaper for the dining area? I will completely agree with whatever pattern and color you decide."

And so that is how it went with the renovations of the old inn—working together every day until late in the evening. Because of the inn's history, they had decided at the outset to keep it looking rustic. As far as their boys were concerned, Thomas and Sherman enjoyed the renovation process. This, of course, was when they were not making deliveries at Walker's. The boys helped their parents take out old wood and other scraps. Handful by handful, they heaped everything into junk piles near the street. Carmen and George gave them twenty-five cents per hour for their work. Each boy said they were either saving the money for college or instead something from Beth's Bakery. Right at the outset, their parents had to make an agreement with the kids concerning how they worked. If an argument broke out between the brothers, some of their money was deducted from that day's earnings.

Eventually, after several weeks of hard work and sore muscles, the Tinkers could now look around and feel that they accomplished their goal. Although casual, the place looked good and very inviting.

One evening, the sunset made a beautiful glow through the restaurant windows, which Carmen was washing. She was standing halfway up her short stepstool, with paper towels and window cleaner in her hands. It was one of the last tasks before buying food for the menu selections. Her back was toward George who was reading from a county government handout. The handout was about scheduling a health department inspection. Placing the informational flyer down on the counter, he looked up at Carmen who was finishing the last window and said:

> "The next thing we better do is make a call
> to the county offices for a preopening restaurant
> inspection. It shouldn't be a problem. I think we
> have thought of everything. I mean, this place is
> clean and neat."

Adam checked his watch and thought that even though it was almost 5:00 p.m., maybe the county office would still be open. After making the call, they were pleased that the health inspector could schedule an inspection for the very next day at 10:00 a.m. With one last look around the place, they gathered the boys. Both brothers were already curled up and sleeping like puppies in the bay windows. George picked up one boy and carrying him in his arms, Carmen took the other. They placed the brothers in the back seat of their pickup truck and headed home.

Neither parent could sleep very soundly that night. Their minds were racing with anticipation for the next day's health inspection. Eventually, they fell asleep for a few hours before the morning sunshine found its way through their bedroom window and onto their faces.

Now that Tuesday rolled around again, besides the day for the Walkers to receive shipments, it was also grocery delivery day at Walker's. First thing in the morning, Carmen placed the boy's bikes in the back of her old Chevrolet pickup truck and drove her two sons and their bikes to Walker's. She had enough time to get back to their new business before the health inspector was to arrive. When she pulled into the stone parking lot of the restaurant-to-be, the inspector, who standing outside their restaurant, was already introducing himself to George. He looked like a nice man, about their own age. Carmen pulled into a parking space, set her pickup truck hand brake and said a little prayer. Feeling a little more secure after talking to God, she opened the truck door and hopped out onto the gravel. As Carmen walked up, she noticed the health inspector had a clipboard with a list of things to check. With a handshake, he said:

> "You must be Mrs. Tinker. Hello, I am Charles from the Food Protection Section of the County Health Department."

Charles tucked his clipboard under his arm so he could shake Carmen's hand while he said:

> "The items on this checklist are requirements by the state of Maine. Why don't we get started? First of all, for my report, let me make sure I have the correct name of your restaurant. I have the name as *Tinker's Country Kitchen,* is that right?"

Over the next half hour, Charles walked around the restaurant's entire interior. He ran the hot water in the kitchen sink, taking its temperature with his pocket thermometer. Then he checked under the sink with his flashlight, then opened and closed all the doors leading to the outside. He even went into the basement storage room. Every so often, Charles made a checkmark on his form or wrote a comment. Once he was satisfied with the interior, he said he was ready to inspect the exterior of the building. At both doors, Charles got down on all fours and checked the thresholds to make sure they were tight when the doors were closed. He knew a tight threshold would help keep any outside rodents from entering. George and Carmen walked close behind him like newborn chicks following their mother. Holding his brown Masonite clipboard, Charles made his finial note and said:

"Okay, folks, let's go inside so I can review my report with you both."

George went in first and cleared a table for all three of them. Once seated, the Tinkers silently held their breaths. Charles seated himself on one side of the table across from both of them. He turned his clipboard around so that they could read his report right side up. He must have done this many times since he could read the report accurately even though it was facing upside-down for him.

"Mr. and Mrs. Tinker, this is a nice, solid building, and you have done a marvelous job restoring it. However, as you can see on my report, there are several things that will need to be corrected before you open up. I will go over all of these with you…item by item.

"You have only one sink in the kitchen—you need a three-basin sink. The first sink is to remove food waste from the dishes while washing. The second sink is to rinse, and finally, the third is to submerge the dishes into a disinfection and drying solution.

"I noticed you have a thirty-foot-deep hand-dug well in the backyard behind your barn for your water supply. We will need to test for any bacteria in your well. Our lab performs tests for total and fecal coliform and also incubates a water filtrate for a standard plate count. A lead test will also need to be performed. You don't want any lead in your water. Your biggest expense will be these next two items.

You need to replace your current water heater so it can deliver hot water at the correct temperature for dishwashing. That old refrigerator must be replaced with a commercial variety that can keep temperatures at forty degrees or below at all times."

Charles paused for a few moments so they could assimilate everything he read to them. He watched for their expressions as they reread the report. When George and Carmen looked up, he gave an understanding glance.

"Finally, you will need to purchase three fire extinguishers and a box of disposable hairnets for kitchen workers. Your north door needs a new threshold, and the pipe chases need to be sealed at the point where the pipes come through the walls. This keeps any crawling bugs from entering your kitchen from outside.

"The good news is that the dining room is fine. As you can see, we are mostly concerned with the kitchen. That is where any food contamination could occur. You certainly would not want to make anyone sick from eating at your restaurant."

Carmen responded, "Oh, absolutely not. Besides being a warm and inviting place for our customers to eat, we want it to be wholesome, clean, and food safe."

George nodded an agreeing yes, and Charles continued, "By the way, this is not an item on the checklist, but everyone working in restaurants must practice excellent personal hygiene including lots of handwashing. If any of your staff become sick, they must not work until they are well again. Sneezing and things like that can spread food-borne illnesses."

Charles remained sitting there with the Tinkers a little longer, then asked if either of them had any questions for him. A rush of panic went through George's body as he looked at Carmen. To his great relief, by this time, she just looked a little glazed, and said nothing more.

"Okay, then, if one of you would please sign the report at the bottom, then I will be off to my next inspection. By the way, later on, if you do happen to have any questions, you can leave a message with our secretary at my office during normal business hours. My unit's telephone number is on the back of your copy."

Charles then took the report from them and separated the original from the carbon copy, giving George theirs. Standing up, he extended out his arm for a handshake and said:

> "Very nice to meet you both, and good luck with your new business. Here also is my business card. Call me when all these items have been fixed, and I will stop by for a final inspection. If everything meets state sanitary standards, I should be able to give you a permit to open at that time."

George and Carmen watched as Charles drove away in his white county car. Both were a little deflated, but they knew each item needed to be addressed to his satisfaction. Carmen turned to her husband and said:

> "Hopefully with God's blessings, we will be able to get all of these problems corrected so our dream restaurant can be opened soon."

CHAPTER

22

Keeping the Peace

Sheriff Jake liked his work, and he liked the people of Port James. One thing about his job was that almost every day's activities were different from the previous day's. Since nearly every shift could be different, he never knew what to expect, sometimes even from minute to minute. Giving out traffic violation citations was never fun, but generally, it was not very threatening. In fact, many times after stopping a driver for a violation, which resulted in giving a ticket, the driver would say they were sorry.

However, most police officers will say that responding to a domestic dispute is the hardest task. They never know what to expect, and many times, their own safety was at risk. Emotions were always elevated, and sometimes distraught people in the home were arguing with a knife or gun in their possession.

To Sheriff Jake, today seemed pleasant enough. The weather was comfortable for him to perform his walking patrol, and residents were going on with their business as normal. Jake felt for a few coins in his pocket and decided he had enough for a fruit turnover at Beth's Bakery. Since he did not have his linen hanky with him today, he had to remind himself to ask Beth for a paper one. Jake opened the bakery door and was instantly greeted with the delicious aroma of freshly made baked goodies. The aroma was a wonderful mixture of sticky buns, frosted cupcakes, fruit pies, and bread fresh from the oven.

With flour on her apron and on her hands, Beth was wheeling her cooling rack to the front of her bakery near the entrance door. The cooling rack was made of six open metal shelves stacked on top of each other, and at the very bottom, there were four little black wheels. When she saw Jake come in, she pushed the rack into its place and said:

"Hi there, Jake, good as usual to see you.
How was your weekend?"

"Pretty fine, Beth. I am just finishing my backyard brick patio and can't wait to start enjoying it with the family. I think they are looking forward for me to start using the charcoal grill again for a nice chicken barbeque meal. I know how to make some great sauce, and it seems that it is my family's favorite. It's a sweet sauce made with honey, ketchup, and some mustard. Hey, Beth, could you save me that peach pie so I can pick it up after my shift?"

"You got it, Jake. It's all yours. I will put your pie in a box and write your name on the top. How about a blueberry turnover today?"

"Beth, you always know how to read my mind."

Placing the turnover in a waxed paper bag, she handed it over to him. Jake reached for a paper napkin from the counter and put one in his pocket. Beth made the change and handed it to Jake with an unusual expression of seriousness on her face. Jake instantly picked up on it and asked:

"What's the matter, Beth? You look like you
have something important to tell me."

"Jake, you know that young boy, I think his name is Zinc... Zinc Bitter. He must be eighteen years old but looks much younger. He always looks so malnourished. A few weeks ago at church, I noticed he had bruises all over his face. I mean, it was at a distance because I sit up front in church, and he always sits in the back all alone. Jake, I am really afraid that Zinc is being beaten at home...and I believe it is happening by his own father."

Standing squarely face-to-face to Jake, she continued, "During the lunch hour, a number of men from the loading docks come in for something sweet to add to their bagged lunch. It's kind of a normal routine for them. They work with Zinc's father and all agree that he is one of those mean drunks. You know, when some men are drinking too much, they get all sloppy and lovey-dovey. They are innocent but annoying. Then other men get plain mean and are ready to start a fight at the drop of a hat. I don't know what you can do, but I certainly hope you can do something…for Zinc's sake, that poor boy."

Jake reassured Beth he would pay Zinc's father a visit. After a moment for reflection, he turned toward the door and left the bakery. Beth quickly brushed off the flour from her apron and followed Jake outside. Watching him walk away, she composed herself by inhaling a few deep breaths of the morning air. She looked up at the cloud-filled sky, and seeing some seagulls gliding through a single sunbeam, she somehow felt that maybe God had encouraged her to say this to Jake.

Instead of doing his normal walk through town, Jake decided to go down to the loading docks to have a talk with Mr. Bitter. Even though Jake was a well-built man with an excess of arm, leg, and chest muscles, he still worked out with his free weights every night. For his personal weight training, he would alternate exercising different muscle groups.

On Mondays, he worked on his leg muscles, on Tuesday arms, back, and chest. On Wednesdays, he did aerobics to build up his lung stamina. This involved running in place or jump roping. Thursday was devoted again to his leg muscles, Friday once again for the upper body strength. Saturday was a rest day, and Sunday was religious devotions for his soul. Not that he only thought of God on Sundays, for he prayed a lot during his patrol. He always prayed that he would do the right thing for his community and do what God would have wanted him to do. It was always reassuring to Jake that he knew his Creator walked with him every day.

Jake was uncertain how to approach this task at hand but decided he had to head directly to the dock master's office at the piers. Hopefully, the dock master had a few minutes to talk with

him. Maybe he could even call Mr. Bitter from his work so Jake
would be able to speak to him face-to-face.

Walking down Third Street, Jake could see the various offices
at the docks. Just past these offices, ship's cargo was being unloaded
and reloaded onto trucks bound to various destinations. Beyond this
activity was the great blue ocean, holding a cluster of white sailboats
between its waves.

It took only fifteen minutes or a little less for Jake to arrive at
the dock office. Taking a minute outside the door, he rehearsed in his
mind what he was going to say.

With three knocks on the dock master's door, Jake opened it
and went inside. Through the salt-sprayed office window, Jake could
see more clearly the activity of loading and unloading wooden skids
of produce from the boats. From this vantage point, he could then
see the skids being taken by forklifts to delivery trucks waiting at the
staging area near the parking lot.

At the far end of the room, he saw Sam, the dock master, looking over his paperwork. A brass gooseneck lamp with a sixty-watt
lightbulb illuminated his desk. Each skid that was unloaded from
the boats was recorded on his paper manifests, making a small stack
in his desk inbox. Sam took care to record each his manifests, and
the boat's record had to match. Showing respect, Jake waited, and
eventually, Sam looked up. He recognized Jake but did not know his
name. Speaking with a gravelly voice, Sam said:

"What can I do for you, Officer?"

"I would like a word with one of your employees. His last name
is Bitter. I hope not to take much of your time or his."

Raising the subject of Mr. Bitter, Sam visibly had bad feelings.
Without any hesitation at all, Sam replied:

"That guy! His first name is Marvin. What
kind of trouble has he gotten into again? I have
saved his job so many times. He gets drunk on
the job, and many of his coworkers just stay away

from him. He has started fistfights with nearly everyone. Marvin even attacked me once, right here in my office...just about where you are standing now. The fact is, last week he didn't even wait for lunch to get drunk. He showed up an hour late all in a mess and drunker than a skunk. I sent him home for his sake as well as his coworkers. I told him he had five days to get sober before showing up for work again. Not that I am looking forward to it, but Marvin should be back at work tomorrow."

When getting information for police reports, Jake found it really interesting how sometimes being silent was the best approach. It always surprised him how people would freely offer more information for him that maybe they would or should otherwise. That was okay, for it made his job that much easier.

Jake could have stayed longer in Sam's office, but he had heard enough. Marvin was rotten to the core, and besides, he knew what he did to his wife about eighteen years ago. Unfortunately, what Marvin did to his wife was not reported, so it did not become a police matter. Then too, eighteen years ago, Jake was only a rookie who was trying to understand the ropes and human nature. Police training for new recruits was good, but not like real life.

Thanking Sam with a handshake, Jake turned and left Sam's office. Walking away from the dock area, Jake knew this may be one of those domestic disputes that no officer looked forward to. Without wavering, he headed directly to Marvin's house. Along the way, he said a prayer for guidance and felt the strength of God going with him.

It was a fifteen-minute walk, but Jake made the trip in five. It was all uphill from the docks, but he wasn't even feeling winded. He knew, though, that the adrenaline in his blood was preparing his body for what he may need it to do. When he was nearing Marvin's house, Jake slowed down and then paused for a few minutes. Both his instinct, training, and experience on the job reminded him to stop and look for anything unusual on the property. He looked for any movement and listened for any noises or voices. Everything seemed quiet and normal. Walking up Marvin's three concrete stairs, he found no doorbell or knocker to use. With the side of his fist, he made seven or eight loud bangs on the door and waited.

A few years ago, while on a police call, he stood at a similar front door. He had heard the faint click of a gun being readied and instantly jumped to the side, narrowly missing the bullet that went squarely through the door. This time, however, he stood front and center waiting for the door to open.

From inside, Marvin unlatched the door and opened it to the light. He squinted at Jake and said, "I hope this is important, Mr. Bigshot Police Jerk, I am a busy man."

With the force of a bull, Jake grabbed Marvin's hand and pushed him into his dark entrance way. With the same powerful motion, he slammed closed the front door, making a thundering noise.

"Mr. Marvin Bitter?"

Marvin responded with a nod of his head, his own hand being crumpled by Jake's giant grip. The pain was so intense that he went to the floor, now on his knees and unable to move. Bending over Marvin, Jake said calmly:

> "Mr. Marvin, have you been beating your son, Zinc?"

With that question, Jake twisted Marvin's arm, making him roll from his knees to his right side. Marvin felt Jake's force tighten even more.

"Can you hear me, Mr. Bitter? Are you abusing your son?"

Marvin squeaked out a faint reply: "You are killing me."

Jake kept up the unbearable pressure on Marvin's body and continued:

> "If I hear about anymore abuse toward your son, you will have another visit from me.

Understand? Think about another visit from me,
it won't work out nicely as this one."

With that, Jake gave one more twist to Marvin's arm, then turned around and opened the door as Marvin was left withering. With a departing kick to Marvin's side, he left him half inside and half outside his door's entrance.

CHAPTER

23

Doing God's Work

After that horrible encounter with his father, Zinc unfortunately knew he had to get away from him and the only house he knew. The only solitude Zinc had at home was his almost totally empty bedroom. At least in the past, his father offered that one place for Zinc to retreat. This time, however, he couldn't feel safe even in his own bedroom. With a little renewed strength, Zinc cautiously ventured into the kitchen. Passing his father's bedroom, he could see that the only one in the house was himself. Walking around in the kitchen, Zinc pulled any canned goods he could find from the kitchen cabinets and threw them into a pile on the dirty yellow kitchen floor. He also found some empty jugs, which he filled with tap water from the sink and added it to the pile. He didn't know how much time he had but decided to take a chance and retrieve his father's suitcase from the basement. It only took fifteen minutes for Zinc to leave his house with the suitcase filled with supplies.

Years ago, Zinc would go down to the railroad yards to watch the individual train cars being pulled or pushed into order by a small train engine called a switcher. He could spend hours there watching the organization of railcars. He often wondered where each train would be going and wished he could go there too. One day when he was there, a torrential rain developed that seemed to come from nowhere. Zinc was sitting next to a railroad shack that was once used to store equipment. He saw the door was unlocked and opened a crack. By a nudge from his shoulder, he got into the shack and out of the rain.

Now, years later, Zinc felt this old railroad shack was the only place where he could stay for a while. In his weakened state, he headed that way with his bundle of food and water. Trailing his suitcase behind, he made it down the front steps and onto the village streets. The last person he wanted to encounter was his father, who by this time, was most likely coming back from the loading docks. Maybe he would have stopped in at one or more bars for some *well-deserved* whiskey. Marvin would always rationalize his whiskey reward somehow. Zinc knew from experience that if he looked at his father for too long when he staggered into the house, he would also get a reward—a hard slap across the face.

So now in his frail state, even though it would be a hard climb, Zinc continued on, pulling his supplies with him to the railroad right-of-way. The right-of-way was elevated so the trains would be at bridge level crossing above Orchard Street. The narrow bridge carried only one set of tracks but made for one less street-level railroad crossing with automobiles.

From this higher elevation, Zinc prodded along the rail tracks, looking for the shack just ahead. Was it God's guidance? Was it an answer to Adam and Silvia's prayers? It surely did not seem to be the 5:00 p.m.-passenger express train came rumbling through just as Zinc followed the railroad tracks onto the train bridge.

With horror in his soul, Zinc turned around to see the train coming toward him at full speed. Were his ears not working? How could he have not heard the tons of metal barreling toward him, seconds away from crushing his poor, weak body? Even with his failing state of mind, Zinc knew he would never be able to save himself and his suitcase. With his last amount of strength, he jumped off the track and pushed himself onto the sidewall of the bridge with just inches between him and the speeding train. With the thundering train noise surrounding him, Zinc couldn't hear the faint impact of his suitcase being completely demolished by the tons of locomotive.

Neither the train engineer, the conductor, nor any of the passengers were aware of the boy's near miss on the bridge moments ago.

Just seconds after the train devoured his suitcase, no identifiable parts of the case were ever found. After a full minute, the speeding train had traveled far down the tracks, leaving only bits and pieces of trash on the rails.

Zinc remained clinging to the edge wall of the train bridge, frozen with horror. His head was still pounding from the deafening noise of the engine and passenger cars. Spent diesel smell permeated his lungs. Poor Zinc looked down onto the cars traveling below. His eyes could not focus. His weakened mind made the street appear to wave back and forth like a rope caught in the wind. Then without even more than a whimper, he collapsed backwards onto the track once more. Black unconsciousness took the pain away from his lack of nourishment and his near brush with death.

Hours later, a light mist was bathing the village as the rising sun shot streams of color into the sky. Birds were once again taking to flight from trees after their evening rest in their nests. Zinc opened his eyes, feeling somewhere between life and death. To his right was the bridge wall where he had clung onto. Was it minutes ago? Was it hours ago? The cool mist brought him back to some form of reality. Pulling himself up, he stood for a while, testing his legs and feet for life. He had no justification to get back to the village, but had nowhere else to lead his body.

He pulled his way off the bridge and slid down the elevated right-of -way onto the village sidewalks. The ability to walk had long disappeared, and poor Zinc had to succumb to crawling slowly along. He did not even know *where* he should go or *why*. With his muscles severely dehydrated and malnourished, he crawled along the sidewalks until he fell face-first onto the recessed entrance of Adam and Silvia's market.

Inside their store, Silvia was humming contently while turning on lights in the market. After she switched on the ceiling lights, she started to clean the counter next to the cash register with her damp cloth. It was 5:00 a.m., and Adam was upstairs in the kitchen while Walt was still in the bathroom. Silvia casually looked out the market door window and then saw the lump of helplessness just outside the store entrance. She threw her cloth down on the counter and ran to open the door. With horror in her voice, she screamed upstairs to Adam:

"Oh my God! Adam… Adam, come down
here quick!"

Adam was finishing his breakfast cereal when he heard Silvia with her frantic voice screaming his name. He swallowed his mouthful of brand flakes and ran down the stairs taking them two at a time. Without slowing at all, he ran through the aisles and tore outside where he saw Silvia bending over Zinc. Silvia glanced up at her husband and, with terror in her voice, said:

"Oh, Adam, I can see him breathing, but
when I whisper his name to him, he doesn't seem

160

responsive at all. Zinc... Zinc...can you hear me? Poor child of God! Zinc? Adam, help me bring him inside! Do you still have that folding camping cot in the back storage area?"

Hearing the commotion, Walt raced down the stairs and into the storeroom. Moments later with the cot under his arm, he ran up to the front of the market.

Walt unfolded the cot and opened it up just to the right of the door near the endcap of the first aisle. Using his left hand, Adam supported Zinc's neck, which seemed limp and lifeless. With his right hand, Adam carefully slid it under Zinc's body, then lifted him onto the cot. Adam was aghast at how lightweight the poor boy's frame was.

Within a half a minute, Zinc was resting flat on the cot with the Walkers around him. Adam bent down on his knees next to Zinc. He cupped Zinc's head with his hands on either side of the poor boys' face. Walt watched as his dad rubbed his hands on Zinc's caved-in cheeks, trying to get any response. Slowly, a little life came back, and Zinc opened his eyes, trying to focus. Adam and Walt went to each side of Zinc and carefully helped him to sit up. Zinc looked at their faces and simply said:

"I am awfully thirsty...do you have some water?"

Silvia was now holding Zinc's hand and, with a nod of her head, motioned to Walt. Quickly, Walt went upstairs for a cup of water from their kitchen.

∞

So as it came about that what was supposed to be a typical, routine morning, God asked the Walkers to take care of one poor child of His. One day lead to another, making weeks pass. Over the next entire month, Zinc stayed with the Walkers, gaining weight and strength. They kept and cared for him like a member of their small family.

Throughout his recovery, Walt shared his bedroom bunkbed. Eventually, Zinc was strong enough to get out of the lower bed on his own. With his generous nature, Walt even gave Zinc some of his clothes to wear. Looking through his clothes closet, Walt turned around and held up several shirts for Zinc to view. Sitting on the edge of the bunk-bed, Zinc could see that Walt liked solid-colored, light-pastel shirts of blue, yellow, red, and green. Walking over to Zinc, Walt said:

"I have a number of shirts. Why don't you pick three for yourself?"

Living with his father, Zinc only had one worn-and-torn brown shirt and a gray T-shirt. He looked at the beautiful-colored shirts in Walt's hands. They reminded him of some sails he has seen on the boats fluttering above in the wind and seeming to float on the ocean water. After a moment, Zinc said:

"I don't feel worthy of such a gift. I just couldn't—"

Walt stopped Zinc's response by placing three long-sleeved shirts on Zinc's bony left shoulder. He looked into Zinc's tired eyes and said:

"No more discussion, Zinc. You deserve them, and they are yours."

Ever since Zinc's appearance on their market's outside landing, Silvia made sure that his stomach was kept full and that he showered every day. After the second week of his recovery, Zinc acted like an abandoned, stray puppy whom someone took into their home. During that time, Zinc followed Walt around all day. However, after learning some of Walt's tasks, he offered to pull his own weight and eagerly helped out nearly everywhere.

Just after dinner one evening, Walt and Adam performed the routine of making the dining room table into the pool table. As father and son started to arrange the billiard balls, Zinc sat in the bay window looking on. After prepping his cue stick with a blue chalking square, Walt asked:

> "Say, Zinc, would you like to join us in a game? Have you ever played pool before?"

At first, Zinc could hardly believe it. In school, Walt was two years younger, but much more popular. All through high school, Zinc never had enough energy to play sports like Walt. Unlike the other jocks at school, Walt would acknowledge Zinc while passing each other in the halls. He always treated him like a human being, one of God's own.

Several times in the past while sharing supper conversation, Silvia or Adam talked to Walt about relationships. Just recently, Silvia had said to Walt:

> "Many children, as well as full-grown adults, sometimes don't think about why an individual is so withdrawn or looks so malnourished. We sometimes just believe that those people are happy that way. We just do not give it any thought that they may be carrying an awful burden."

Pastor Westman once preached on that very subject. His title was *Just Who Is Your Neighbor?* After church on that particular Sunday, the Walkers talked about his sermon over a Yankee pot roast dinner. Yes, Pastor was right: our neighbor is *anyone* who needs our care and help.

Now, by caring for Zinc, the Walkers were living their faith, not just professing it in a shallow way. Helping someone may not be at a convenient time in our lives, but we are called to help.

Since Walt asked him to join them for pool, Zinc stood up from the bay window seat and touched the side of the table with his fingertips. Adam walked to Zinc and offered his stick to him. Surprising as it was, Zinc did better than holding his own at billiards. He actually cleaned up. Both Adam and Walt could not believe their eyes as one ball after another found its pocket. Walt turned around to his mother who was finishing the dishes in the kitchen area across the room and said:

"Hey, Mom, if Zinc could be my pool partner in next month's Port James billiard competition, can we keep him?"

Zinc beamed at Walt's bit of humor and wished it could be true. He desperately wanted to be part of a group—a team where he would be valued. For any organization that would allow him to be part of, Zinc knew he would give his very best effort. He just had to be given the chance to be a real member of a team. In many ways, the Walkers were a team working well together. With much admiration, Zinc felt *that* was something he could only dream about.

Adam took Zinc's cue stick and placed it placed it against the wall. He then paused for a moment before saying, "Silvia, Walt, Zinc, I have been thinking about this for a while. We need to have a family meeting and now is as good of a time as any."

Adam walked over to the couch, taking a folding chair with him. The time had come when a decision had to be made. He sat on the metal chair while Silvia, Walt, and Zinc found places on the couch. Adam glanced at Zinc who was looking down and rubbing his hands quietly together. Adam cleared his throat a few times then started to say what was on his mind:

"Zinc, soon after you arrived at our doorstep, you told us that your father probably did not know where you went or even cared. The three of us certainly feel that you were right. Now that it has been a little over a month. Have you contacted your father?"

Still looking downward at the floor, Zinc responded, "No, sir, I haven't. I have thought about that nearly all the time. The truth is… I'm afraid if he knew where I was, he would bring trouble to me… and probably even to your family."

Silvia touched Zinc's shoulders, which were looking a little fuller since their caregiving. While taking some time to think, she then said:

> "Zinc…honey, look up at me. We would love to have you stay with us. You have been nothing but a joy to have around. Your help at the market may even allow my husband and me to take little vacations here and there. You and Walt work together so well."

Walt nodded in agreement but was wondering where this conversation was going. Never having a brother or sister, Walt embraced Zinc like his very own kin. Adam then picked up where Silvia left off in the conversation:

> "Zinc, have you ever thought of enlisting into the army? They need good men like you. We understand you are now eighteen, and so you do not even need your dad's permission. You may be able to learn a trade. After four years, when you get out, you would be able to make a good income, totally separate from your father."

Having this talk with Zinc, Silvia and Adam went downstairs and then outside to sit on the back loading dock for some fresh air. Zinc remained on the couch, looking at the wall across from him. With the thought of joining the Army, he felt a little more energized. Maybe it would be good for him. Certainty, it would fulfill his life-long desire to be part of a team. Tonight, he would pray about it just before going to sleep.

That evening, Walt laid in the upper bed of his bunkbed, thinking about how to improve his pool game. While half asleep and half awake, he heard Zinc whispering a prayer:

> "Dear heavenly Father, thank you for having this wonderful Walker family who restored my health within a totally safe environment. Just as important, thank you for their love. Almost a month ago, I believe you have guided me to them. I don't know what plans you have for me, but maybe Mr. and Mrs. Walker are right. Maybe I should join the Army... I have always wanted to be a member of a team. So, dear God, just please guide my path in the direction that would be the best for me. I love you and thank you for your goodness. Nevertheless, whatever is your plan for me, I will accept that Your will be done. Amen."

Walt thought how easy it was for Zinc to pray. It was as if he was talking to a real friend—well, it was, a heavenly friend.

The next morning for breakfast, Zinc brought two bowls of cereal over to the couch for him and Walt. After finishing half of his cereal, Zinc put his bowl on the coffee table and said:

> "Walt, I thought about what your dad said regarding me joining the Army. I think I want to give it a try. I hope you don't mind me asking, but would you allow me to borrow your bike? I believe the recruiting office is located somewhere inside the county office building down on West Road a few miles."

Walt placed his bowl along with Zinc's on the table. "Sure, bro, I won't be making any deliveries today, so it is all yours. I left the bike on the back loading dock."

Zinc thanked Walt and picked up his cereal bowl to finish his last few spoonfuls. They both sat on the couch together in silence, wondering what the future would bring.

Within an hour, Zinc was pedaling towards the United States' Army recruiting office just outside of town. After his brisk trip, Zinc road up to the front of the building. It was surprisingly a large and imposing building considering the size of Livingston County and Port James. He pushed the bike into the rack near the entrance, took a deep breath, and went up the twelve steps to the inside. The floor was marble, and as Zinc walked, it made a hollow sound with each of his footsteps. It reminded him of the sound of marching soldiers.

The Army recruiting office, which was really just a desk and two chairs, was located in far the corner of the county office building's lobby. When Zinc stepped up to the recruiting officer, the soldier, wearing a smart, well-pressed army uniform, stood up and gave Zinc a hearty handshake. He offered Zinc a seat, and they conversed for a few minutes. Zinc was surprised how approachable the officer was with him.

Eventually, the officer gave Zinc some brochures for him to look through. There he sat on the wooden seat in front of the officer's desk, looking through five brochures to see what the Army had to offer enlisted boys. Zinc just superficially glanced at each, then asked the officer where he could sign his name to enlist.

෯

It was not more than two weeks later, and the Walkers were standing on the train platform with Zinc, waiting for the 5:00 p.m.-passenger train to pull into the station. It was the very same train that nearly killed him earlier. That horrible incident was just over six weeks ago.

After fifteen minutes of waiting, Zinc and the Walkers could hear and then see the diesel locomotive coming into view about a quarter mile up the tracks. Pulling the six passenger cars and a mail car, the train took only a few minutes more to arrive at the Port James Station. From the depot platform and down a little ways, a handler grabbed two large canvas bags of mail and swung them up into an open door of the slightly moving mail car. Inside the car, a U. S. postal letter sorter stood behind a long table, organizing letters into five or more sacks.

Nearer to Zinc and the Walkers, the conductor, who was still on the train, opened the passenger car door while at the same time adjusting his black visor hat. Just as the train made a full stop, he started down the steps, carrying a portable yellow stool. He knew to locate it in place since the first step on the train was so high. From the platform, Zinc couldn't hear anything through the train windows although he did look through the one directly above and in front of him. Inside the train, a six-year-old child was happily running up and down the center aisle with her teddy bear in arms. Her older brother was seated with his parents, reading a picture book and eating some Ritz crackers. Watching that fleeting scene, Zinc wondered if he would ever be blessed with his own wife and children—a real family of his own. Blinking his eyes a few times, he turned around and looked at Silvia, Adam, and then Walt. Without any words, the four of them went into a group hug. After an additional squeeze, he wiped a tear from his eye and proceeded to the train car steps next to the conductor who punched his ticket and handed it back to him.

Inside the train, while looking for a seat, Zinc thought how ironic it is that instead of ending his life, this same train just might be taking him to a better future in the United States Army. Although the Walkers had a lot of misgivings, they hoped and prayed that the Army would serve Zinc well. Watching Zinc leaving for the unknown life in the Army, Silvia said a quick prayer, "Please Jesus, be with this boy. Keep him safe and keep him close to you always. Let his faith in your saving grace never waver. Amen"

Now seated, he looked at his dear friends through the window and waved as the train engineer released the air brakes, making the train move slowly forward and away from Port James.

Our God surely works in mysterious ways.

24

Success

Even from the very first day, the Army was great for Zinc. All he had to do is everything the drill sergeant yelled at him and his new recruits to do. Zinc never flinched when the sergeant got into this face. Growing up with his father, he was used to all that kind of treatment. The real difference, however, was that Zinc knew all this Army training was designed to be good for him. It would eventually build up his character and make a man out of his empty shell. Private Zinc had a perfect attitude for the Army. He developed both in body strength, endurance, and self-esteem. After finishing the ten weeks of Basic Combat Training at Fort Jackson, South Carolina, he asked the drill sergeant how he could get into the welding school program.

Because of Zinc's personality, respect for his superiors, and endless desire to work hard, his name was forwarded to his lieutenant with highest recommendations. Within days, Zinc was sent to Advanced Individual Training (AIT) for welding. Besides learning to weld, which even included underwater welding, he had to pass Basic Structural Engineering, which included algebra, differential equations, then applied calculus.

Zinc literally and figuratively sweated over this, but so did everyone else in his class. The difference between him and his classmates was that when they went out to have a few beers, he stayed back at the barracks, drinking awful-tasting coffee and poured over his books.

Ten weeks later, to Zinc's own surprise, he placed the highest in his class for the academic portion of the instruction. Over the next eight weeks, learning the actual "hands-on" welding techniques was exciting for Zinc. With every new welding skill that he learned, Zinc made sure he remembered everything he could, reviewing his previous notes and Army handouts. Finally, on September 10, the test for his actual welding skills was conducted for this select group of Army men. For Zinc and everyone else in his class, the test was incredibly difficult, mentally as well as physically.

Wearing all his welding gear, they sat him in front of several kinds of metals, including black iron, aluminum, and steel. Zinc literally sweated continually under his welding mask for the entire grueling eight hours. He had to properly match the correct welding rod and proper gas supply with each metal that was to be joined. Selecting the proper welding temperatures was also critical so there would not be any metal burnout but still hot enough to melt the weld material. Each of his finished welds had to be twenty-four inches long and the welding marks nice and even. When all the metal joints were finished, they were graded on the appearance, tensile strength, and compression strength. His metal joints were tested and found to be superiorly made. He had placed first in his class for both academics *and* first for technical welding abilities.

❧

True to Army protocol, a graduation ceremony announcement was posted on the main cork bulletin board. Attendance was mandatory for the whole company, not just the graduates. Dress uniform was required for the ceremony to be held the following Tuesday, at 1530 hours.

The graduation ceremony was dignified, exhibiting *Army smart* and precision. On stage, Zinc received his certification with a snap from his captain's salute. With Army perfection that was drilled into him, Zinc returned his salute and marched off the stage, a full-grown man with pride in his heart. This pride came from his newly mastered welding abilities and pride for his United States Army. The graduation was rather short since only seven men had completed the requirements. After a few words from the captain, the graduates and the rest of the company were dismissed.

Even the Army Sergeant knew there was a place and time for his men to enjoy levity and share with each other their congratulations for hard-earned accomplishments. As the men gathered in the dining hall that was set up for visiting family and friends, the atmosphere became more relaxed. A few of the graduates unloosened their ties and folded their hats over their military belts. One by one, the graduates found their families and greeted them with hugs and kisses.

Zinc was truly happy for all of them but knew this would be a letdown for his spirit. There was no one in the mess hall for him to receive congratulations and a hug. Through the crowd, Zinc saw his sergeant leave the building and go outside. After a few minutes, he came back into the building and went directly over to Zinc. Looking at Zinc straight in the eyes, he said:

"Specialist Bitter, I am giving you an order.
Please join me just outside on the north lawn."

Zinc followed, then releasing himself from all Army display, and broke into a full run. Right there on the lawn waiting for him were the Walkers. As soon as they saw Zinc, they started jumping up and down waving hands with unmatched joys of excitement for their Army man. Without slowing down, Zinc ran into hugs and pats on the back from Silvia, Adam, and Walt.

Three days earlier, the Walkers had closed the market and made the car trip just for him. Through flowing tears of joy, Zinc said:

"God bless you! Thank you! I love you!
Thank you all for being you! Thank you for all
you have done for me...and thank you for coming to see me!"

They couldn't stop hugging their friend, and Zinc couldn't stop hugging them either. The direction Zinc took and his accomplishments were truly God's work in his *and* the Walker's lives.

For the remaining afternoon, Zinc showed them around his barracks, the education building where he took his welding test, the chapel, and the callisthenic building. Toward evening, it became time for the Walkers to go back to their motel. Zinc walked with them to their car and had one more hug. As Adam put the car into gear, Zinc watched his friends, all waving out the window. Soon, their car was at the checkpoint after a few minutes, the gate was lifted, and they were gone.

⃠

The next day, on the drive back to Port James, Walt and Silvia took turns riding in the front seat, making conversations with Adam. Adam insisted on driving the entire way back home even though it was somewhat monotonous. He liked to talk about the scenery as he drove, but toward evening, with less to see along the way, Silvia knew it was more important for her and Walt to engage Adam so he wouldn't get drowsy behind the wheel.

After six hours of driving, they stopped for petrol at a rural gas station. Walt changed seats with his mother and used the bench seat in the back for a bed while she moved up front. Silvia looked at her husband—gosh, they had been married for sixteen years. He was forty-one now, and his jet-black curly hair was starting to get white around his temples. In silence, she thought how it made him look more distinguished. He truly was a handsome man and perfectly suited for her. Ticking off the miles, Adam glanced at her for a moment and asked:

> "Hey there, woman of my life, what are you thinking?"

Silvia was caught a little off-guard with his question but answered him truthfully.

"Adam, I was just thinking that at first, I loved you for your innocence. Now through the years, I love you for your dedication to our marriage and your wisdom and faith in God. I have seen how splendidly you relate to our son and recently how much you have cared for Zinc."

Adam was pleased with her thoughts. After a few more miles, he said with a grin, "Is there anything else, Silvia?"

Moving a little closer to Adam so she could whisper in his ear, she said:

"Of course, there is more, Adam. You are handsome and are very macho!"

Adam pulled his head away a few inches in order to see her in in full view from his right side. She didn't always talk like this, but he loved it even though it was unexpected. Silvia checked to make sure Walt was asleep in the back, then she pulled closer to his ear again. To his surprise, instead of whispering, she started to nibble on his earlobe with her front teeth.

From sheer excitement, Adam tightened his grip on the steering wheel while his heartbeat quickened. Then Silvia whispered:

"Really, Adam, and I truly mean this. Any woman would love to have you as their husband. I am grateful for you in my life. You are God's gift to me."

Correspondence

It had been three full years since Zinc's first day in the Army. He was a man in his own positive environment. He couldn't get enough of military life. In fact, as much as he wanted to see the Walkers again, it truly was three whole years before he came back to Port James for his first leave after enlisting. Maybe not coming back home to visit was partly due to having to contend with his father.

Throughout the past three years, all correspondences from Zinc were to the Walkers. In many ways, he felt that they were his family, totally the opposite of what he thought about his father. Unlike all the other men in his Army unit, he never knew what happened to his mother. He had no childhood recollections of her, not even how she looked. Zinc had no memories of her singing lullabies at his bedside before falling asleep. There were no perfumes that reminded him of her. He didn't even know the color of her hair or how she styled it. For some mysterious reason, his father kept this a total void in his life.

For Zinc, growing up as a child, Aunt Rhonda, who was widowed and lived nearby, would come to the house and take care of necessities. She was a stocky woman with a heart that felt obligation to Zinc and her brother, Marvin. Zinc did not feel any motherly love from her, but she was kind to him. She made sure the laundry was done and a dinner was prepared. Just before Marvin came home from work or the bar, she made sure Zinc was okay, and then quickly left to go to her own empty home. Feeling her age and waning energy, his aunt Rhonda continued this until he was only ten years old.

Throughout the early years of his life, this was Zinc's home life. Empty of family but although meager, having sustenance enough to manage. Years before Zinc was born, his father fell more and more into his downward spiral. Zinc knew even before the tender age of seven years old to keep his distance from his father, especially when he came home from the docks. He always did his homework all by himself. It needed to be done first thing after school and then put away. If his father saw his homework on the table, Marvin would mock him, calling Zinc a teacher's sissy.

ஐ

So now with months coming and going in Adam and Silvia's married life, years passed and the month of May was crossed out on the 1955 calendar. Summer in Maine had arrived once again. At their market, local squashes, tomatoes, and even some cherries were displayed for sale on Adam's outside fruit stand. The smell of fresh fruits and vegetables from the produce stand was its own best marketing. Most bus commuters would buy something fresh from Adam's stand to pop into their brief case or brown paper bag for lunch.

Over the years, by one in the afternoon, Silvia fell into the routine of looking for William, the mailman. Each and every day, the time of his mail delivery for the market wavered only a few minutes. Today, he had another letter from Zinc for the Walkers. Postman William handed the letter to Silvia and commented with a smile:

> "I just happened to look at this letter with the Army return address. It is from Zinc. I know he writes every week, and from what you tell me, the Army is treating him well. The next time you write him, could you say I say hello?"

Silvia took the letter from William's outstretched hand, together with a Sears Roebuck and Spiegel catalogue. Balancing the heavy bundle of mail in her arms, she said to William:

> "I sure will write that you give him your best regards. Right now, William, if you have a minute to spare, I'll read this letter from him out loud for you."

Turning toward the back of the market and waving Zinc's letter back and forth, she announced, "Hey, Adam… Walt! Do you want to hear what Zinc wrote this week?"

Adam was adding some more paper bags to the hook in the ceiling for his customer's line of credit, and Walt was cleaning the coffee grinder. Both came to the front of the store to hear Silvia read:

Dear Family,

> Thank you for the updates from around town. I am glad your market is still doing fine. You mentioned that Thomas and Sherman are continuing the grocery deliveries to the home-bound customers. That is such a win-win enterprise. It is teaching great responsibilities to the two boys and gives you time for the market chores. Of course, your customers probably love the energetic lads.
>
> In your last letter, you wanted to know when I would be able to come home for a visit. You said for me to always think of your apartment as mine too. Well, I have exciting news! The Army has given me a 30-day pass to come back home next month. I can't wait to see you all! I hope I can take you up on your invite so I can stay with you.

God willing, I will see you in three weeks
on June 21ˢᵗ.

Love and hugs,
Zinc

Silvia placed the letter down on the counter next to the cash register and exclaimed:

"That silly boy…asking if he is welcome to
stay with us! Of course, he is welcome!"

Before Silvia started reading Zinc's letter, William had set his well-worn leather mail pouch on the floor. Bending down to pick it back up again, he said:

"Adam, after Zinc arrives, are you going to
have a homecoming party for him…and invite
all of us?"

With authority in his voice, Adam answered, "Of course we will… I mean…won't we, Silvia?"

"Oh, Adam, you don't have to ask, of course, we will, and I know just where we will have it!"

Zinc Back Home

The repetitious rocking back and forth of the passenger train would normally lull many riders asleep, but Zinc was an exception. Watching the changing landscape through the train's window, Zinc felt his excitement grow within his heart. Traveling closer with each mile, he thought about seeing his Walker family again. It even surprised him how his desire grew more and more with each mile closer to Port James.

The military kept Zinc on the go from early-morning revelry to early-evening taps. There was Army calisthenics, which helped to increase body strength, flexibility, and fitness, followed by mundane barrack duties, and finally practicing his welding trade. The reality was that he had very little time to think of anything else except Army. Because of his welding skills, he was sent on three tours of duties to Korea. He volunteered for the third one. There he repaired tanks, jeeps, and an assortment of other large military pieces of equipment. He didn't even know what some of the equipment was used for, but he really did not need to know. He was one of the best welders the Army had and was in great demand.

With his train coach seat reclined back, eventually, Zinc did nod off. Sometime later, the train conductor walked down the aisle and announced the next stop.

"We will be arriving into Port James in twenty minutes. For those passengers leaving us, please take all your luggage from the overhead racks. There will be a fifteen-minute stop at the station. Port James… Port James…next stop."

Zinc retrieved his Army duffle bag from the above rack and sat back in his seat, watching some familiar buildings come into view. It was a few minutes past midnight, and he was wondering how long it would take to walk home to the Walkers from the train depot. He also wondered if anyone would be awake at their apartment. Maybe Silvia would still be up, waiting for him, but probably asleep on the couch.

As the train started to slow, Zinc could see that a heavy drizzle of rain was coming straight down from the dark sky. Maybe he would get a taxi so he could keep his Army uniform dry. Hopefully, he would be able to wait for it just inside the train depot.

Preparing to arrive at the station, a few other train passengers were getting their belongings together. Along with them, Zinc maneuvered from his seat to the center aisle while the train was pulling in for the stop. The line of people slowly shifted past each seat to the far end of the train car. Now with the train completely stopped, the conductor opened the door and jumped onto the depot platform to place the yellow stool. One by one, passengers went down the steps to the depot platform. The conductor was there helping anyone who needed a hand. Janet, a little girl with her panda bear, was sound asleep in her dad's arms, her brother stumbling along behind his mother. As Zinc descended the train's three steps, with total surprise, he nearly dropped his duffle bag on the concrete depot platform.

There, waiting through the rain drizzle stood not just the Walkers, but also Pastor Westman, Beth from the bakery, and Sherriff Jake. George and Carmen Tinker were also there with both of their boys. Thomas and Sherman were holding a homemade sign in their little hands, now a little wet from the rain. Printed on brown cardboard from a produce box, using colorful crayons, they had written, "Welcome Home, Zinc. We Love You!

Zinc was completely overwhelmed. Aside from the Walkers, he had no idea that any other villagers cared about him, until now.

Despite the late hour and the cold rain, this small group gathered at the train station platform just for him.

God was good.

Not wanting to miss anyone, it took a while for Zinc to individually thank and hug everyone for being there. Each had smiles and congratulations for him. The Walkers waited until the small group dispersed, then they walked with Zinc to their car in the parking lot. While Walt and Zinc climbed into the back seats, sitting in the front, Silvia turned around and said:

> "Zinc, we hope you will stay with us during your stay. Feel free to visit friends or do whatever you like. Don't think you need to work at the market unless you want to."

Zinc thought just for a split second and answered, "Thank you, Mr. and Mrs. Walker. I would love to stay with you. I would find it a privilege to help out at your market. Besides, there is one thing I have missed like crazy. I want to spend a few minutes each morning at your third aisle and smell that fresh coffee from that coffee bean grinding machine! Army coffee tastes and smells like dirt!"

Walt then added, "Zinc, I have been waiting for over three years now to beat you at billiards. You better save some time for me. I have a new cue stick, so I just might clean the table on my first turn like you had done to me so many times!"

Zinc looked at Walt and said with a grin, "You can bet on that, bro. I have been busy lately and did not have much time for my game. So you are on, you might even win a game!"

Sitting in the front car seat, Silvia looked at Adam and whispered, "It is good to have him back."

It was only a five-minute drive from the depot to the market. Arriving at the back loading dock area, Adam parked the car and set the brake. The four of them piled out and stumbled a little going up the back wooden stairs to their apartment. Conversations had to wait for morning since the hour was late, and everyone was tired. Zinc looked around and realized how much he missed their place and his "family."

In the morning, the next day, before the boys woke up, Silvia and Adam had already showered to the singing of another opera from their neighbors. They were dressed and already in the kitchen. Zinc slept late for the first time in years, and it did Silvia's heart good to know that he actually slept in. Putting some bread in the toaster, she said to Adam who was reading the morning paper:

> "I need to take a few hours off from the market this afternoon. I have a meeting with Carmen at their restaurant to finalize things for Zinc's welcoming home luncheon next Tuesday. I should be back by four o'clock…possibly even sooner than that."

Adam stood up and walked to the kitchen drawer to fetch a butter knife. Getting some grape jelly from the refrigerator, he then took out his toast from the toaster, and said:

> "I thought we decided to have the pulled pork sandwiches Carmen told you about during coffee hour after church last Sunday."

"Oh sure, but we also need to pick out sides, what to drink, and some sort of dessert. After that we should be all set."

◦

Tinker's Country Kitchen had been open, serving lunch and dinner for more than three years. George and Carmen had their yearly health department inspection with Charles. This time, it was last Wednesday. It went flawless, and as usual, Charles had no violations to write on his report. Their menu is simple for lunch, and every evening, they offered a special, besides their regular entrees.

Just before one o'clock, Silvia hung her beige apron on a hook on the back wall of the market by the door to the loading dock. Adam was replacing a light bulb above the same door.

Touching his shoulder, Silvia said, "Okay, dear, it's time for me to drive to Tinker's restaurant to talk things over. I'll see you a little later."

With that, she fussed with her hair a little as she moved past him. Pausing for a few seconds, she asked Adam, "Darling, yesterday, did you fill up the car like I asked?"

Adam gave her a thumb's up and said, "Sure thing, my little lady. I take good care of you!"

Just before opening the door, she gave her little finger wave of approval—just for him.

Once in their car, Silvia pulled down the visor and checked her hair and lipstick once more in its attached mirror. Driving to Tinker's Country Kitchen, Silvia wondered how their restaurant business was doing. In a few minutes she drove into the parking lot and noticed that it was empty, except for Carmen's old pickup truck. Through the front bay window of their restaurant, Carmen saw Silvia drive up from the road. Pulling off her kitchen worker's hairnet, she walked out to greet her.

"Hi there, Silvia, come on in. To go over details, we can sit nearly anywhere you like. Let me get you a cup of coffee. Do you take cream and sugar or take it black?"

It didn't take too long for Silvia and Carmen to decide on a nice menu for the party. Silvia gave Carmen the total number of people attending and made a check out for the costs. While handing the check to Carmen, Silvia asked:

> "So how is business going, Carmen? Whenever we come here for dinner, your food is excellent, but Adam and I always notice a lot of empty tables, even on a Friday."

Coming from the kitchen and into the dining room, George walked over to join the women. Wiping his hands on the front of his apron, he then shook Silvia's hand. Carmen explained to George:

"I was about to tell Silvia how our restaurant business is doing."

Having a much more serious expression than just before Silvia's question, she continued:

> "This is certainly something we have prayed about a lot, and especially lately. Silvia, we love this business. After all, it is our dream. As you know, we both quit our jobs to start the restaurant. We had to take out a business loan, and right from the start, we used a lot of that money to update our kitchen. To save some cash, we did much of the renovations ourselves. It's not as if we will close any time soon, but every month, expenses are more than what we make for that same time period.
>
> "Well, enough of that. We are trusting in God, and He will show us the way. Be assured, we will do a lovely job for your luncheon. It will be a very nice time that everyone will remember fondly. George and I are really looking forward to this, and by the way, we want to thank you once again for thinking of us to host this event for Zinc."

Silvia looked at both of these people who were so dedicated to the church. She saw them every Sunday singing in the choir. Unknown to anyone, they gave more than they should to the church, but that was just the way they were. Sometimes they called it *blind faith* or *childlike faith, simple and true.*

Silvia started to extend her arm for a handshake but decided that she wanted to do a group hug instead. With their heads together and arms around each other, Silvia said a prayer for them:

> "Thank you, God, for the blessings you have given all of us. We ask that you give this family an additional measure of your guidance and help them in ways that you only can possibly know. In Jesus's name, we pray. Amen."

The Party

For many servicemen and women, coming home after three years of military service, one more year to go meant a nice welcoming from their families, but not necessarily a luncheon. The Walkers knew Zinc would not have a family other than what they provided him with. Then too, Zinc had come so very far from the brink of mental despair and physical demise. They wanted to do this for Zinc, and so did many other Port James residents.

The Tinkers outdid themselves at their restaurant. On the center of each table, they arranged a small bouquet of blue forget-me-nots with a miniature American flag. There were crepe paper streamers flowing in arches from the ceiling. George found several records of John Phillip Sousa marches to play on his portable record turntable.

Even though all thirty-five people attending paid a set price for their meal, the Tinkers added more from their own personal expense to the food buffet. George was available at a hand-carving station to serve a standing rib roast and glazed ham. Besides the tomato-based pasta, grilled chicken, potato and vegetable salads, and homemade rolls, Carmen bought special Italian cookies from Beth's Bakery.

The best part of all this was that all during his luncheon, Zinc appreciated every single detail. When he entered the front door of Tinker's Country Kitchen with the Walkers, he was speechless. Then he could not stop thanking everyone. The festive decorations and the special food was a treat for the attendees, but one look at Zinc's expression as he entered was priceless.

Zinc wore his Army brown dress uniform. His perfectly pressed light-brown shirt and black tie was nicely visible with his V-cut jacket. On one side, the jacket displayed his patch for engineering and welding. His trouser legs with its hard creases ended just above his spit-polished black shoes.

Even though overwhelmed with emotion, standing there for a few moments, Zinc could hear parts of several conversations about him:

"What a handsome gentleman!"

"I can hardly recognize him. Look at his broad shoulders and perfect posture."

"How about that million-dollar smile... I wonder if he has a girlfriend."

"I need to introduce him to my daughter right away!"

After many handshakes, and when all the guests were finally seated, Adam stood up and asked Pastor Westman if he would offer a blessing. Everyone quieted down and folded their hands.

"Thank you, heavenly Father for this young man, Zinc. He is a perfect example of showing grit determination, along with his love for you. We humbly ask for you to continue guiding Zinc in everything he does especially while he is away serving our country. And please keep him safe from any danger or harm.

"Thank you for the friendship in this room that we have for each other and for a secure place to raise our families. George and Carmen have worked tirelessly on this luncheon, and we also give thanks to them. Please bless this food to the good of our bodies. Amen."

With the prayer ended, George called the tables two at a time to fill their plates at the buffet. It was a wonderful event, and the Tinkers enjoyed it as much as anyone. They arranged it so the restaurant was temporarily closed for regular customers. "That way," said Carmen, "Zinc's guests could stay as long as they wanted."

After the dessert of Italian cookies and coffee, and a few hours of conversations, people started to say their goodbyes. When the last guests had left, except for the Walkers and the Tinkers, Sherriff Jake took advantage of the moment to talk with Zinc.

"Hey, my friend, some party, huh?"

Zinc always had respect for the law, but he now had a greater appreciation for Jake's work. Maybe Zinc's appreciation came from his time in the military. He remembered gathering in the center courtyard outside of his Army barracks with the rest of the soldiers. Standing on a raised platform overlooking his men, his captain read each soldier's name over the loudspeaker. After each name, their deployment destination was given. No one even thought to protest; it was their duty. Nearly all the young men were being sent to Korea.

Zinc caught himself as he had been lost in his thoughts for a minute, but then said to Jake:

"I'm sorry, sir. I was thinking of something else just now. Yes, it certainly was a surprise, and a nice party for sure."

Sheriff Jake took on a serious look, touching Zinc's arm while he continued:

"Zinc, would you be willing to shadow me tomorrow on my foot patrol through Port James? There may be a few more people who would want to say hello to you…not everyone could make it this afternoon. It would also give me a chance to talk with you some more."

Jake had thought about having this talk with Zinc for many years, even before he joined the Army. Although there was never a perfect time to tell him, Jake believed that Zinc was ready and strong enough to hear what he had to say.

With a little hesitation, Zinc said, "Well, sure, I have the time tomorrow, and I think I would like that a lot."

The Truth Be Told

Both Walt and Zinc woke up to the breakfast aroma of frying bacon coming from Silvia's kitchen area. Sitting on the couch, Adam was already showered and dressed and was reading the morning newspaper out loud to Silvia. Not being able to sleep anymore, both boys put their bathrobes on and went single file into the hall toward the living area.

Adam looked up from his newspaper and greeted the boys, "Good morning, sleepyheads, did you sleep well?"

In kind of a unison chorus, they both said they slept like a rock. They were almost ready to sit on the couch when Silvia said:

> "You fellows must have stayed up late play-
> ing pool. As you know, I gave up trying to keep
> awake until midnight. Now, gentlemen, if either
> of you want breakfast, you better change the pool
> table back into the dining table quick and fast."

Folding the morning newspaper back in the way it was before he started reading, Adam thought he would add his comment too and said to the boys, "That's an order and do it on the double!"

Once breakfast was done, Walt and Zinc went back into their bedroom. Walt said, "Would you like to shower before me or some-time later?"

Zinc slipped off his red pajama top up over his head and took a folded shirt from the upper drawer of the dresser. Thanks to the Army calisthenics, his arm and chest muscles were firm and generous in size. As he fastened the first button of his shirt he said:

> "After the last game of pool that I beat you at, you went straight to bed, but I didn't follow you. Instead, I took a shower. I knew I would not have the time for that this morning. In about ten minutes I'll have to leave. Sherriff Jake wanted me to accompany him on his rounds around town."

Going through his clothes in the dresser Walt replied, "Wow! I'm impressed! Going around the town with Sherriff Jake is so really cool! Let me get some of *my* best clothes for you to wear. Maybe passersby might mistake *you* for *me*. They would be so impressed…especially with the girls my age. When you get back, tell me all about it."

Zinc was waiting for Jake outside Barton's Hardware, next to the lamppost that twenty-two years ago, Adam had used to practice his opening conversation with Silvia. Looking West on Maple Avenue, Zinc could see Sheriff Jake approaching as he walked. When Jake got near Zinc, he said:

> "Hi there, Zinc, I am glad that we will have this time together. First, let me treat you to one of Beth's apple turnovers."

As they went from business to business, Zinc noticed both a friendship and respect everyone extended to him. Every day even though Jake only stopped at each place for a few minutes, it was surprising how much he knew about the families, both good and bad. He also was continuously scanning the street for anything that seemed out of the normal course of things. At one of the Victorian homes that still stood amongst the village businesses, Jake paused for a moment and placed his hand up to his ear.

"Hear the dog barking in that home on Orchard and Fourth? The one over there with the new roof? That nice home is own by the Davidson's."

Zinc had to strain to hear the dog. He figured it might be a larger breed due to its low bark.

"Now that you mentioned it, yes, I can hear him or her."

Jake continued, "That is Kenny, and he is a Golden Labrador Retriever. Three weeks ago, I heard him barking, but it just wasn't his normal bark. It was high-pitched. I decided to walk over to see if there was anything amiss. It didn't take long for me to see smoke coming from their partly opened kitchen window. See, the Davidsons had left for work at 7:45 a.m. like I know they always do. They generally give me a beep on the horn when they drive pass me while on my walking route. So because of this routine, I knew they both had left the house.

"I didn't know this, but on that particular morning, since they were in a hurry, they forgot to turn the stove off when they were boiling some potatoes. In not much time, it could have started a fire. Because of the barking dog and the smoke, I quickly ran up to the home. The front door was locked, so I went to the back door and found that it was unlocked. Swinging the door open, I entered inside and followed the smoke to their second-floor kitchen. The room was starting to fill up with smoke, but I caught it just in time. I pulled the pot off the stove and pushed it into the sink."

"Wow, sir, it sure was good that you were so intuitive."

"Well, Zinc, that's my job. See that white bench just ahead? Let's sit for a while, I need to tell you some things."

By now, Zinc had the feeling that what was coming next was the real reason Sherriff Jake had asked him on his foot patrol.

"Zinc, I need to tell you some things about your past that will make you upset, but you need to know the truth. Do you want me to continue?"

Zinc took a deep breath and nodded for Jake to go on.

"Twenty years ago, before you were born, your mom and dad were very much in love. They settled in this area, living in the beautiful home that your mother inherited from her family. Everything seemed to be working so nice for them until your dad started to drink. It could have been because he lost his job…that is just hearsay. For whatever the reason, he became depressed and, at first, starting drinking in the evening, then soon after…nearly all day.

"Your mom had no idea how to deal with a man who seemed to love his bottle more than life itself. She retreated into her own space, using her only hobby she knew just to make it through the day.

"Week after week, turned into months, and he would be gone for almost all that time. Zinc, please don't judge your mom when I tell you that she had a month-long secret affair. She really loved the man, and from that love, you were conceived.

"When Marvin came back home, he could see that your mom might possibly be pregnant. He went into a drinking rage, blaming your mom for everything. Months later, when it was time for your mom to deliver, she had to drive herself to the hospital. Meanwhile, when she was in the hospital, back at the house, Marvin destroyed the only thing that made her happy. He physically smashed the thing to pieces with an axe, making it a pile of debris on the floor. Then he smashed it again and again until he went out for a well-deserved drink.

"When your mom came home from the hospital, instead of having the joy of her newborn, she completely lost it. There on the living room floor was what was left of her vintage upright piano.

"Like a perfectly orchestrated plan, Marvin was there with some transport staff from the county mental hospital. Viewing her rage was all they needed to take her to be committed by her husband. See, for the previous two weeks, every day, Marvin had visited the director of the mental hospital, telling him lies, terrible lies about her instability. He said she was dangerous to herself and was afraid of his own safety.

"Again, Zinc, I can't emphasize that these were all lies. I have more to tell you Zinc. Are you still able to hear more?"

Zinc had to hear the rest no matter what the truth was. He shook his head *yes,* and Jake continued:

"Back then, some mental hospitals prac-
ticed backward ways to control their patients.

Some poor souls were kept in isolation for weeks, others were denied food. Worse yet, some were given electroshock therapy to their brains or even an operation called prefontal lobotomy. That means they surgically removed the connective nerve tissue between the two sides of the brain. It made the patient into no more than a vegetable. Fortunately, your mom did not have any of that done to her. She was, however, not released from the mental hospital until eight months later. The whole experience really scared her. Some say she has never been the same.

"When she was released from the mental hospital, Marvin was waiting for her at the hospital gate. He told her that he still hated her and that he was taking her son to live with him in a nearby apartment. If she ever tried to communicate with either of them, he would kill her.

"Zinc...this poor, misunderstood woman is Lady Remington...your mother."

More to Come

The next day at the Walker's, without saying much during breakfast, Zinc went downstairs and through the market to the village streets outside. One place he could feel alone with his thoughts was on the hill of Gray Cliff lighthouse.

Being in a strange daze, his legs headed him toward the lighthouse. Zinc went through the motions of walking, but somehow, he didn't feel that he was connected with his body. Without even knowing how he walked the short distance to the lighthouse, he sat on the grass and stared at the ocean breakers rolling into the rocks. To say the least, he was reeling from all the family history that Jake had told him yesterday at the park bench.

He knew Sheriff Jake was right. He had to know what had happened to his mother. Then too, maybe a few years ago, he would have not managed well about learning all this. Now, with three years in the Army behind him, he was a strong man who could handle it. But was he really able to? Would he fall apart again, being no better than Marvin? He needed to talk with someone. Should it be the Walkers? Maybe Adam or Silvia would listen, but then Walt was closer to his own age.

At the lighthouse, Zinc looked at the world around him; it was still good. He also realized how many people cared for him and his well-being. Sitting there next to God's nature, he felt a calmness enter his soul. It wasn't like the clouds in the sky opened up and a voice from God talked with Zinc, but he sensed God's presence in a real and true way.

Way down on the sandy part of the shore, Zinc could just make out the sandpipers scooting along and poking their beaks into the sand to eat shrimp. Sometimes they traveled along the wet portion of the beach in a line; then other times, they patrolled the beach alone. Within a few seconds, they would regroup and start the procession once again. Zinc remembered Pastor Westman preaching from Matthew chapter 10, verse 29. He said our God cares for his creation so much that He even knows when a mere sparrow on earth passes from life. Zinc thought that if God cares so much for his birds, then how much more must He care for him.

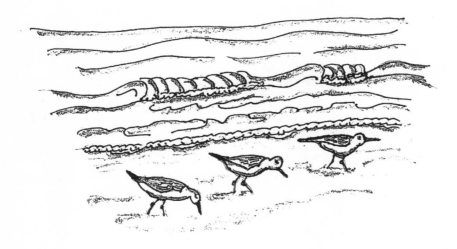

After sitting in the grass for an hour or so, Zinc felt that God was somehow telling him to get up and find Pastor Westman. Feeling a little more refreshed, he stood up and brushed off the grass and sand from his pants. Because it was Saturday morning, he knew Pastor would be at the church. He also remembered that about this time on Saturdays, pastor would be teaching confirmation classes in one of the Sunday school rooms. Turning around to look out to sea one more time, he started down the path into the village. Zinc could just see the top of the church steeple where the church was located on Maple Avenue and Third Street, a few blocks away.

It didn't take too long for Zinc to reach Our Lord's Lutheran Church. He distinctly felt God was giving him strength and direction, but for what, he did not know. From the door nearest the parking lot, confirmation students, Bibles in hand, were filing out of the church. Zinc walked up and held the door open with his outstretched arm. Once inside, he headed to the pastor's office. Pastor Westman looked up from his desk just as Zinc appeared at his door. With a sincere pastoral look of concern, he said:

> "Hi there, Zinc, nice luncheon you had the
> other day. Come on in. Is there something I can
> help you with?"

"Hello, Pastor, I am not really sure. I just felt something inside my heart that was directing me to you. Although confused…here I am."

Pastor Westman took some time to reply, trying to understand why Zinc may be confused. He thought it may be something about his father, but he wasn't positive. Still standing just inside the office doorway, Pastor could visibly see Zinc was in some distress. Thinking a few moments more, Pastor said, "Zinc, please come in and have a seat."

Pastor Westman motioned him to an overstuffed chair in his office. Zinc paused for a moment as if undecided to do so but then walked to the chair and sat down looking at the crucifix on the wall above Pastor.

"Zinc, I have to believe this is more than a coincidence. It could have been our Lord directing you. See, I have scheduled with the head nurse at City Hospital to visit your dad. I was just ready to pack things up to leave when you came in the door."

Pastor got up from his desk, placed some papers in his out basket, and walked over to Zinc. Now standing close to him, Pastor Westman said in a soft and concerned tone:

> "At church last week, your aunt Rhonda asked
> me to pay your dad a visit because he is not doing
> well. She is not sure if you knew about his con-
> dition, or even if he ever wrote to you. She gave
> your dad your army address. Zinc...do you feel like
> coming with me on a pastoral visit for your dad?"

Zinc couldn't help but think about the only other time he went with a professional. That was Sherriff Jake, and he wondered if this would be as dramatic. How could it? Zinc stalled for a moment, thinking about how to respectfully decline. He then thought of all the soldiers, including himself that obeyed orders and went to Korea.

"Yes, sir, I will go with you...and thank you for the offer. No, I did not know Marvin was in City General Hospital."

ဆာ

During the thirty-mile car trip to the hospital, Pastor Westman wanted to ask Zinc why he referred to his dad as *Marvin*. He had heard a dad being called by his first name before, but Zinc seemed to say his name with a certain amount of distain. Or was it pain? Pastor measured his timing, and after a few minutes of silent driving, he asked:

> "So may I ask you, Zinc? Is everything okay
> with you and your dad?"

Zinc looked out the side window watching the landscape pass by. He had a flashback of his beating but quickly pushed it from his mind and said:

> "Marvin and I don't see eye to eye, and he
> drinks a lot. He treated my mom horribly not to

JAY DIEDRECK

say how he has treated me. Since leaving home to join the Army, we have not written or communicated in any way. And, Pastor, he is not my biological father."

Pastor Westman sensed that there was a deeper problem between them, more than with what Zinc just said. He gave pause and quietly said:

"Zinc, I have seen how you have grown over the past few years, and all for the better. However, if you ever want to talk with me, you know how to reach me. Sometimes I can offer some help, sometimes I can just listen, but we can always pray together."

Nothing more was said between them until they pulled into the main parking lot entrance of the hospital. Looking out his side car window, Pastor Westman said:

"It seems like this place is building something new every time I come here. Look over there, they are adding a whole wing onto the side of the building. Pretty soon there will not be room for parking. Of course, most of my hospital visits are back at our local hospital in Port James, so I don't need to come here more than a few times each year."

Pastor drove around the parking lot a little more. He came up to two parking spots that had a sign in front of them that read, "Reserved for Clergy." Pulling into one of the spots, he placed a large card on his dashboard that indeed stated, "Clergy." He explained to Zinc that it keeps him from getting a parking ticket.

It was a walk of a few minutes from the parking lot to the visitor's entrance. As they walked together, Zinc felt a looming sensa-

196

tion of uncertainty. He had no idea how this meeting with his father would go, but it couldn't be good.

Once they came to the automatic double doors, Pastor Westman stepped ahead, leading the way to the visitor's desk in the lobby. There was no one in front of them, so they walked right up to the receptionist who greeted them with a smile. Viewing the black and white clericals that Pastor was wearing, she said:

"Hello, Father, can I direct you to a specific patient area?"

Although he was not called *Father* in the Lutheran church, he didn't mind. She had a printed name tag on her blouse that read, "Mrs. Davis, Volunteer." Pastor thought how wonderful that there were people like her who freely gave their time to work in the hospital. Smiling back at her, Pastor said:

"Yes, Mrs. Davis, we would like to visit a patient named Marvin Bitter."

It took a few minutes for Mrs. Davis to look through the admitting records for Marvin Bitter. Without success, she then asked her coworker for another notebook, which was red in color. She looked up at the pastor and Zinc and said:

"I am sorry for the misunderstanding. I was looking in the wrong admission folder... I see your friend is listed here as a patient in our intensive care unit. When you get to that unit, check with the head nurse. Usually, they only allow one visitor at a time, but since you both are clergy, they will probably let you visit together. Here are directions to ICU."

Zinc and pastor found the unit after seeming like they walked for over a mile. It was a maze of corridors and stairwells. The closer they got to the unit, the more activity they encountered. The ICU was near the emergency entrance of the hospital. On a wheeled bed, a patient was being rushed past the admitting desk and right into surgery. Pastor and Zinc instantly moved over to the wall, making enough clearance for them.

Pastor found the head nurse station and, within a minute, was directed to room 17. The nurse's station was situated in the center with the twenty patient rooms around the edge like a circle. Trying not to stare in the rooms they walked by, they finally arrived at room 17. Zinc immediately froze when he saw *Mr. Marvin Bitter* written on a card on the outside of Marvin's room door. Pastor turned to Zinc and saw his expression. Touching his shoulder, he said:

"It's okay, my friend. I am with you, and more importantly, so is Jesus."

Zinc was not prepared for what he was seeing. Marvin was sitting up in the hospital bed. He was attached with clear tubes going to each arm, and another one actually went into the side of his body. There were monitors surrounding him that were recording his vitals such as oxygen level and heartbeat.

An oxygen mask was hanging from Marvin's face, close enough to put back on quickly yet low enough for a nurse's aide to spoon-feed him. It looked like she had some brown baby food in a small cup.

As soon as the aid noticed them, she placed his oxygen mask back on Marvin and, standing up, pushed her stool away with her feet. Looking at the food cup in her hand, she said:

"You can come closer. Right now, it doesn't look like he wants anything to eat."

Zinc moved over to be closer to Marvin. He was so pathetically skinny. His skin was so thin that his bulging blue veins could be seen all over his body. His complexion was colorless, and his hair was just a little fringe around his head. Just past his blistered lips, Zinc could see a remnant of some teeth, if you could call them that. The few that were left were yellow-gray and crooked. Marvin's glassy eyes were fixed on him.

Something came over Zinc. Maybe it was due to Marvin's condition, or maybe it was from not seeing him for three years. Whatever it was, Zinc stretched his right arm so he could put it around Marvin's back and give him a hug.

With a total misunderstanding, Marvin instantly stuck out his own hand in an effort to protect himself from what he thought was going to be Zinc's direct hit to his face. Zinc caught Marvin's frail hand. He held it in the air for a split second, then carefully lowered it back down. He gently pulled his father's head and shoulders away from his hospital pillow and turned it into a hug. Although Marvin's eyes filled up with tears, it was Zinc who said:

"I forgive you, *Dad.*"

Zinc held the hug for a while, feeling Marvin's shallow breathing against his chest. He then carefully guided Marvin's back onto his pillow. Zinc felt that his reason for being here was now done.

Looking even more exhausted, Marvin then motioned to Pastor Westman to come close. In a faint whisper, he said:

"Will I go to hell, Pastor? Can God ever forgive me?

Pastor Westman bent down a little so he could look directly into his eyes. Marvin's stare latched directly onto Pastor's.

"Marvin, you have fought your demons most of your life. You have hurt the people that you should have loved. This is between you and God. Jesus took the very sins you have committed in your life to the cross and died there for you. Listen carefully to me, Marvin. Right now, close your eyes and pray to God to forgive all the sins you have done, those you know of and those

which you don't even know. Marvin do it right
now...*right now, Marvin.*"

Marvin closed his eyes and, moving his blistered lips in silence, said a prayer that almighty God in heaven heard. After his lips stopped moving, Pastor Westman moved away from his bed and stood next to Zinc. Both men looked in silence as they watched this failing man. He was a man who failed in life and is now failing physically.

Without warning, the monitors around him started beeping, and Marvin began violently and painfully choking. Some blood came from his mouth as he gasped for air. Immediately, several nurses came rushing in, asking Zinc and Pastor Westman to step outside his room.

Through the window, the men saw the nurses pulling Marvin's neck back. Then they forcefully inserted a breathing tube into Marvin's mouth, pushing it down and into his lungs. It was an effort that was not to work. With the nurses looking on, Marvin gasped three times, then left this world.

Right before Zinc's eyes, Marvin had died. Pastor placed his arm around Zinc and gently turned him around. They silently walked the hospital corridor, away from Marvin.

Once outside of the hospital and walking to the parking lot, Zinc took a few deep breaths. It wasn't until they were back into Pastor's car before he asked the question that was in his heart:

"Pastor, do you think my dad is going to heaven?"

Pastor studied the crucifix that was laying on his car seat between them. He picked it up and rubbed it between his fingers, feeling the likeness of Christ on its cross. With sincerity in his voice, he said:

"Zinc, I certainly hope so, but that was between Marvin and his God."

CHAPTER

30

Helping Hands

From City General Hospital, Pastor Westman drove Zinc directly to Walker's. Nearing the market on Maple Avenue, Pastor slowed down his car.

"Zinc, do you want me to leave you off at the front or at the loading dock around back?"

"Oh, around back would be good. If there is a delivery, I will be able to help out."

When they reached the back of the market, both saw that there were no truck deliveries at that time. Zinc thanked Pastor and reached for the passenger's handle to open the door. Before he had a chance to swing the car door open, Pastor said to him:

> "Zinc, you did well today. I think God gave you the gift to forgive your dad, and I know Jesus was in that room with us. Again, Zinc, you did well—you delivered God's message of love to him."

Zinc would have wanted to spend more time with Pastor, but it was the hour for both of them to go home to their families. Once outside the car, Zinc walked up the three steps of the loading dock. Instead of going through the market's back door, he waited on the loading dock and watched Pastor's car make the turn onto Third Street. Once his car was out of sight, Zinc turned around and opened the door to enter the market.

While cleaning the coffee grinder, Walt saw him first and walked over to greet him as he wiped his hands on his apron front. Extending his hand for a shake, he said:

> "Hey, bro, you have been gone all day. You owe me a game of pool after dinner. Come on in, my mom is making one of her famous meat loafs. She could possibly use help mashing the potatoes. For me, I need to take a quick shower. It's a lot harder to run a business when you are not around."

With that, Walt put an arm around his bro, and together, they walked up the backstairs to the apartment. Silvia was at the kitchen area. Looking toward them, she gave a smile to Zinc and Walt. Adam was reading the evening newspaper while seated on the couch and said:

> "I hope you had a good day, Zinc. Walt is biting at the bullet to play pool with you tonight."

Silvia took the pot of potatoes off the stove and tipped it in the sink to drain the remaining water. Placing it on a trivet, she started mashing the potatoes while adding butter, salt, and a little milk. Zinc walked over to the counter and asked if he could do it for her.

"Great, thanks, Zinc. I'll get the plates on the table. Oh, Adam, could you do your magic and change the pool table into our dining table?"

As usual, dinner was great, and everyone ate more than they should have. Silvia was the first to leave the table and went to the refrigerator. With one hand on the handle, she said, "Has anyone saved room for ice cream?"

The boys stayed seated as Silvia started to scoop out some vanilla into four dessert bowls that she placed on the kitchen counter. Zinc sprang up and started to clear the dinner dishes before Silvia placed the filled ice cream bowls on the table. Silvia said, "Zinc, leave those dishes in the sink. Let's sit down. I want to tell you all something."

Selecting four spoons from the drawer, she sat down and gave one to each of them. Between tastes of ice cream, she said with a smile:

> "I have some great news. Beth's daughter, Nichole, is getting married! For three whole years, Nichole has been working in their family business, *Beth's Bakery*.
>
> "Besides this excitement, she asked me if I thought having the reception at Tinker's Country Kitchen would be nice. I told her I thought that would be just great."

Silvia scooped a little more ice cream into her spoon and continued:

> "It has been quite an effort for George and Carmen to make ends meet. Maybe this is a new venture that may work for them. They could keep the restaurant going and also host wedding receptions or other parties. After all, they did a great job for Zinc's luncheon."

Everyone agreed, and then, with a little more small talk, the family finished their dessert. After cleaning their bowls with their spoons, the dining room table was converted by the boys into the pool table for the evening games.

∞

From the restaurant the next day, Carmen called Silvia on the phone with the exciting news. Beth had asked them to host Nichole's wedding reception. Even though Silvia already knew the Tinker's restaurant would be selected for the celebration, she listened happily. Carmen said she could hardly believe her ears; it must be God's answer to their prayers. The only issue was that the date for the wedding was just six days away, but Carmen told Silvia that she and George were up for the task. After a few more details exchanged, Carmen and Silvia hung up with each other.

The weather forecast for the next week was sunny with a light breeze off the ocean. The high temperature for each day was in the high seventies to low eighties, normal for the end of August in Maine. It would be perfect for their wedding and reception.

The next telephone call Carmen needed to make was with Nichole, the excited bride-to-be. She decided to call her while George was spray cleaning the dining room windows. Nichole was the perfect bride. She knew what she wanted but was kind to everyone whom she hired for various wedding and reception tasks. Everyone loved her too, including Pastor Westman, the staff from the stationary store, Ruth from the flower shop on Third and Oak, and a friend of hers who was going to be the wedding photographer. Of course, their own bakery would make Nichole's wedding cake. She hired music students from Portland to play in a classical string quartet during dinner. She could relate to college students who would jump at making some extra spending money. They asked for a total of 80 dollars, but Nichole said that was too little and secured their services for 120 dollars.

Nichole never went to college, but working in the family's bakery, she had waited on many students. More times than she could count, the students would pool their change together in order to afford a turnover or two to share with each other.

So George and Carmen were flying high. This would be their first wedding reception that they would be hosting. To have Nichole for their first bride was just lovely. They would do a good job for her and her groom, Patrick. It would be an event everyone would definitely remember.

After hanging up the phone with the bride to be, Carmen gazed around the restaurant. She looked at her spiral notebook where she jotted down the wedding reception details. Then she looked around again in hopes of finding George to share her thoughts. Carmen then had a few more ideas that popped into her head. George was in the restaurant's basement storeroom checking inventory when he heard Carmen calling him from the top of the stairs.

"Are you down there in that back room? Can you hear me, George? Are you at a point where you can stop and talk with me? Is that one light bulb burned out down there? Watch your step coming up the stairs. Can you come up here for a few minutes?"

George placed his clipboard down next to the five-pound bags of flour, and with a sigh, he went up the steps where Carmen was calling him a moment ago. George saw Carmen walking around the restaurant, her ideas coming into her head like a snowstorm in January. Glancing at George she said:

> "How about we make a big splash for this wedding? I was thinking of real linen table clothes and tall-stemmed glassware. George, you missed a streak on that last window. Are you using enough clean paper towels? What would you think of real candles at each table, maybe at each window too? Do you think those ceiling beams should be stained a second time? They look uneven again since you did them last. Are they a little wet? I can't tell from here. How much do you think cloth chair coverings for the head table would cost? I think white would be nice… with a generous bow in the back of each chair… maybe beige…no white. Should we wear something a little more formal for this reception? How about my long black evening dress for me? You liked it when I wore it last year at our high school reunion. You couldn't take your eyes off me. Remember how it shows off part of my back

and in the front, the sequins around my neck?
That does it, George, and don't argue with me.
You should at least wear a suit and tie. Maybe the
white tie, no, the red one would be good…no,
the white one. Yes, definitely the white one. Is the
white one clean?"

George's mind was working fine, but about sixty miles per hour
slower than Carmen. Twisting the lead back into his mechanical pencil and clipping it into his front pocket, he said:

"Carmen, dearest, are you sad that we only
have two boys and no girls? No girls to plan a
wedding for? Is that what this is all about?"

"Oh, George, I love our boys and our life. It's just that I love
planning special occasions like these."

ℂ

Even though Carmen was adding more to their tasks and George
was being driven a little crazy by her, they would not even think of
skipping church. So by Saturday evening, four days later, the Tinkers
got their boys into bed early—that is, early for summertime. After
Thomas and Sherman showered and were tucked into bed, having
said their prayers, George and Carmen decided to enjoy a little glass
of wine.

Sitting on their couch, in their upstairs apartment, they started
to hear Lady Remington playing beautiful classical piano music from
the downstairs. To hear her piano playing better, George got up from
the couch and opened the door of their apartment, which lead to the
grand balcony. This evening was Lady Remington's fantasy concert
where she was performing for a full audience in an ornate, baroque,
metropolitan opera hall. For the Tinkers, life was beautiful.

Stealing this time together on the couch were cherished
moments, and they thanked God for them. After an hour and a fin-

ished bottle, they were mellow enough to allow themselves to go to bed. They slept well that evening and didn't even wake up for a few seconds when it started to rain softly, as it made little pattering noises on the outside of their bedroom window.

ℰℴ

Even though the Tinker's normal Sunday morning routine was always tight, during breakfast this special morning, Carmen announced to her family:

> "If we hurry, we have just enough time to
> drive to the restaurant on our way to church.
> I want to make sure everything looks perfect
> tomorrow, for Nichole and Patrick's wedding
> reception."

Her husband and the boys knew that they shouldn't give Carmen any more time to think of anything else, so they quickly made it to the bathroom to brush their teeth. After brushing, George helped each boy to comb their hair. Rinsing each comb in the sink, they both put them in their pockets. Silvia said all little boys should carry a comb and pocketknife.

It only took a few minutes to make the extra swing to their restaurant.

Wiping her side window with her hand, Carmen noticed her fingernail polish needed a little touching up, but that would have to be done later. Glancing over to her husband, she said:

> "Oh, George, I am so excited! This may be the
> big turnaround for our business...and for us!"

Pulling into the parking lot while avoiding the rain puddles, Carmen said: "Everyone stay right here in the truck. I will just be a minute...keep the motor running."

As soon as she entered their restaurant, the family heard her scream at the top of her lungs. George and the boys took no time to pile out of the truck and head to the restaurant door that was still open. Inside, they saw Carmen pointing up at the ceiling. Drips of leftover rainwater were flowing off the center ceiling beams and onto the tables below. Carmen kicked off her high heels so she could move faster and started dragging the tables away from the drips. George and the boys jumped in to help, moving the tables safely away from the center of the room.

Carmen started shaking uncontrollably, covering her face in disbelief. Tears filled her eyes and wetted her hands. Once again, George looked up at the dripping, wet beams, then at Carmen. Picking up her Sunday high heels from the floor, he raced over to his wife and embraced her in a hug. The boys joined the hug, making it a family embrace. Thomas found a folded hanky in his pocket and, raising it up to her, offered it to his mom. In turn, Sherman reached up and rubbed her arm for comfort.

The four of them stood there in silence and with total helplessness. In a weak voice, George finally broke the trance and said to his precious family:

"Let's just go to church and put it in God's hands. Come on, we are needed to sing in the choir, and we all need to pray for an answer."

Slowly, the four left the restaurant and found their places in their truck. Sitting in the front seat and looking straight ahead, Carmen had a blank stare as she said softly to herself over and over again, "How could God do this to us? *How could He do this?*"

࿐

Church was well attended even though it was during the summer months. Pastor greeted everyone with a smile and a handshake as they entered the sanctuary. The Tinkers had to bypass Pastor Westman and enter the building from the side door directly to the choir practice room. The boys found their way to one of the back pews in the church near where Lady Remington was sitting.

The whole service including the choir anthem was nourishing, but the Tinkers still felt ready to die. This was going to ruin Nichole's wedding and most likely end their business once and for all. As usual, Pastor led the liturgy and the congregation sang the Sunday's hymns. When it was time for the pastor's sermon, he read the Holy Gospel from Matthew, Chapter 13. At the pulpit, he opened the Bible and read the parable of the sower:

> Behold a sower went forth to sow; And when he sowed, some seeds fell by the way side, and the fowls came and devoured them up: Some fell upon stony places, where they had not much earth: and forthwith they sprung up, because they had no deepness of earth: And when the sun was up, they were scorched; and because they had no root, they withered away. And some fell among thorns; and the thorns sprung up, and choked them: But other fell into good ground, and brought forth fruit, some a hundredfold, some sixtyfold, some thirtyfold. Who hath ears to hear, let him hear. (Matthew 13:3–9, KJV)

While in the choir during the service, George and Carmen could not talk freely with each other, but they certainly looked into each other's eyes. They both knew that in the parable, the seeds represented faith in Jesus' promise of forgiveness and God's place for them in heaven. The seeds were also those of total faith in God for everything in one's life. Is their family the kind of seed that at first blossomed but then withered when things really fell apart? Could they fall away from trusting in God? After all, all over the world, terrible things happen all the time. This was one of those times, those terrible times. God seemed to turn His back on His trusting family. They were literally ruined.

After the end of his sermon, Pastor Westman asked if anyone had any concerns for the congregation to pray for. Sitting there in God's house, George wrestled with himself. Was this something to ask from the congregation? Would they understand? Was it even appropriate? If he was wrong, then he would have to own it. But if he was right, was there anything wrong with asking for congregational prayers?

George stood up to be recognized by Pastor, but at the same time, Carmen also stood. Together, they explained how the roof was dripping rainwater into their restaurant, and they needed prayers. Pastor turned to the alter and said:

> "Let us pray. Dear heavenly Father, please look down on these, your servants. They trust in you and need your help. We don't know what can be done, but we just ask for you to use your guiding love and place your hands on their shoulders. Please help them to see the right path they need to follow."

At that point in time, Pastor did not know how to help, but by the end of the service, the spirit of *helping your neighbor in need* became a reality. During the coffee hour, the Tinkers were flooded with volunteers. Without knowing what their church friends could really do for them, Carmen said one more prayer to herself then asked everyone for their attention.

"If everyone could just come out to our restaurant, maybe we can think of something...and God bless each one of you."

After arriving home, as quickly as they could, the Tinkers changed their clothes and drove to the restaurant. As soon as they arrived, they saw that other cars were also coming into the parking lot. People were spilling out of their autos and gathering in the restaurant dining room.

Within the group of volunteers, some were talking amongst themselves, pointing up at the ceiling. Others went over to examine the condition of the wet tables. A few of the men went up on the roof to check out the damage. Before doing anything quite yet, George thought it would be best to wait for the men to report back concerning the roof's condition.

Eventually, Frank the carpenter, and three other men came down the stairs after checking out the roof. Wiping his wet shoes on a towel that someone had placed on the floor for them, Frank said:

> "It's really worse than it looks from inside. The roof is nearly flat, and the poor thing just can't keep the rain out anymore. There must be three inches of rainwater collected up there."

Carmen looked to her husband and, almost in a pleading tone, asked:

> "Honey, do you think we could have their wedding reception in the barn out back? Thank God, our kitchen is still fine. If we use the back door from the kitchen, the barn is only a few steps away. Is Nichole here? Does anyone know if Nichole is here? She and her family were in church today. She must be here somewhere. Has anyone seen Nichole?"

Nichole and her family were just driving up through the parking lot. Seeing their car, Carmen ran outside to talk with them. When she got to their car, Carmen looked inside their window and saw that Nichole must have been crying. Without any hesitation, she opened their back door and said:

> "Honey, please don't cry, I know your wedding is tomorrow, but I have an idea. Let me take you to the barn just behind the restaurant."

The barn was totally empty inside and had been updated a few times throughout its hundred-year life. Only four years ago, the previous owners had refinished the wide-planked floors and were in perfect shape. All the windows had also been replaced a few years ago. None of the walls, the towering ceiling, or the beams were ever painted thus, showing its natural wooden beauty. Being post and beam construction, huge timbers reached into the ceiling. Massive tie beams stretched high across from one wall to the other. Lap and pegged joints tied the structure together. Nicole was impressed with its interior but couldn't help seeing the coat of dust covering everything, even the windows.

By this time the whole work party had all come into the barn and were looking all around its impressive interior. Frank stepped in front of the group and said:

> "By golly, we can do it. We have sixteen hardworking people here...*your neighbors*...just like pastor read to us from the Bible a few Sundays ago. First, we can make this barn as clean as ever, then work on getting all the furnishing placed. Decorations should be the last to be brought in and put up."

Zinc volunteered to work on the high ceiling. He could easily climb and work way high on the forty-foot ladder. In Korea, he welded cracks in steel towers that were much taller and during those jobs; he also was wearing his welding mask, carrying heavy gas tanks with him along with other gear.

With a renewed spirit, Nichole looked at the group that assembled to help both the Tinkers and her. With a smile and a flamboyant swish of her hand in the air, she said:

> "Well, let's get going, my friends! We have my barn wedding reception to put together!"

Just after church, Pastor Westman was one of the first men arriving to help. He was wearing shorts and his new high top PF Flyers sneakers. A few volunteers had to take a second look to see if it was him since he was almost never seen *not* wearing his pastoral clericals. While he started washing the barn windows from the outside, he went through his next Sunday's sermon in his head. Whispering to himself, he rehearsed:

> "We know that God listens to all our prayers, and they are answered in His own time and way. It may not be the answers we look for with our prayers. In fact, sometimes we question whether he has heard us at all.
>
> "We must truly understand that he has heard each and every one of our prayers. As we struggle here on earth, we don't always understand God's answers. All of God's answers will be understood only after entering God's heavenly kingdom."

With that intro set in his mind, he smiled and moved his ladder over to clean the next window.

ॐ

On Monday, the day of Nichole and Patrick's wedding, the skies cleared up, and with a cool wind gently blowing, life was worth living. The wedding ceremony officiated by Pastor Westman at Our Lord's Lutheran Church was both beautiful and meaningful. Nichole, accompanied arm-in-arm by her father, processed to the altar while a trumpeter from the balcony played Purcell's trumpet processional. Pastor's sermon message of lifelong commitment was meaningful, appropriate, and well-received. Martin Luther's hymn "A Mighty Fortress is Our God" was sung along with William Walsham's "For All the Saints." After the vows were spoken and Pastor's pronouncing of their marriage, Holy Communion was celebrated, first by the new couple and then the attendees. After the benediction, Nichole and Patrick left the altar, now as a married couple, to the trumpet announcement of Purcell's brilliant trumpet recessional.

Both Nichole and Pastor did not want flash photography during the service, so a reenactment at the altar with the couple and the wedding party was staged for pictures. Family photos were taken on the church steps. It was about one o'clock in the afternoon when the wedding party and family finished the photos and made the car procession to Tinker's barn for the reception.

Out on the nice green lawn in front of the barn, the rest of the guests were being treated with tasty appetizers of light, flaky pastry cups with either skewered shrimp, roasted mushrooms, or a flavorful melody of creamed greens. Carmen enlisted the help of a few young college students who were eager to serve the hot hors d'oeuvres and make some money. She asked them to come dressed with white shirts or blouses and black pants. They did a nice job of mingling among the guests, offering the treats from silver platters that they carried. George had set up a self-service table for red and white wine, beer, or iced water. When the wedding party arrived from the church, the whole group raised their glasses and cheered.

With Nichole and Patrick's celebration in this vintage barn, it was clear how God answered. The lovely and delicate decorations, white linen-covered tables and chairs, and English china setting stood in stark contrast with the barn's majestic construction. The barn's huge timbers towering skyward to the ceiling and the rough walls of wide-planked boards were an inspirational test of time and strength. They symbolically mirrored the blessings of a newly conceived, God-centered holy marriage. The barn's lovely ambiance was truly warm and welcoming for this unique and very special marriage celebration.

As the guests slowly migrated to the barn's entrance, the lovely bride and handsome groom stationed themselves just inside the barn to greet each guest. With a hug and kiss, many whispered to Nichole that she looked breathtaking in her off-white, Chantelle laced dress and plunging neckline. She wore a simple neckless of powdered blue-sea glass that just touched the top of her cleavage. Her dangling earrings were two-inch silver droplets, which matched the silver weave of her bracelet.

Complements were also directed to Patrick, who was wearing a tuxedo with silver-studded cufflinks and a ruffled shirt sporting a powder-blue bow tie. He selected an off-white jacket to match his bride's wedding dress and accented it with a blue-cumber bum that matched the color of his bow tie.

Besides the verbal exchange of these niceties, the out-of-town guests just had to ask why she was so lucky to find such a spectacular and stunning place for their reception. Truly a splendidly perfect choice.

God is *always* with us.

Mother and Son

Tuesday, the day after Nichole and Patrick's wedding, Silvia and Adam were in their kitchen, reminiscing about the beautiful time everyone had. Even Walt said that it was the first time he had seen so many girls look so fine all in one place. Talking to Zinc, he said:

> "Zinc, you were dancing like a pro—the
> women were lining up for their turn."

A little embarrassed, Zinc answered quietly, "Oh, it was just because of the uniform."

The day before yesterday, after they had gotten back from the work party, Zinc asked Silvia if Walt had some Sunday clothes for him to borrow for the wedding. Showing a little perplexing look on her face, she asked:

> "Why wouldn't you wear your Army
> uniform?"

"Oh, I didn't want to draw attention to myself. You know, maybe away from Patrick, the groom."

"Zinc, we are all proud of you. Please wear the uniform. Does any of it need touching up?"

Now, since it was Tuesday one again, deliveries for the market were going to arrive shortly. Adam was finishing his oatmeal and got up to put the bowl in the sink. After filling it with a little water, he turned to Zinc and said:

> "This past month sure has gone by fast! Tomorrow, we will be saying our goodbyes to you at the train station. Is there anything you want to do today—that is, instead of working in the market?"

Zinc had a serious tone in his voice when he answered:

> "Thank you all for being my Godsend. I love you all so very much. The next day after the luncheon you had for me, Sherriff Jake asked me to spend some time with him while on his foot patrol through the village. He told me some shocking news about myself and my family. The following day, you know that I spent the after-noon with Pastor Westman, where I saw Marvin in the hospital. Well, I was wondering if maybe I could ask you for a big favor. Could I borrow your car today—that is if you will not be using it and it is okay? I need to visit Lady Remington."

Silvia answered for the two of them. She placed her arm on Zinc's shoulder and said simply:

> "Of course, Zinc, and if I could ask, will you please deliver her monthly groceries while you are there?"

ଅଚ

At least a hundred times, Zinc thought about how his encounter would go with his mother. That was probably why he waited until the last day of his leave in Port James to visit her. It was not that he did not want to see her; it was that he wanted it to work out in the best way. The Army taught him that. If he followed the Army's set of rules and orders, then there was a predictable and beneficial outcome. It was the same with welding. Using the right welding rods, correct temperature, and proper gas, and of course, skill, the weld would hold tight.

But with this? How will it turn out? How would he approach her, his own mother, his own flesh and blood? The woman who bore him and gave him life?

Adam handed Zinc his family car keys. Seeing an overwhelming seriousness in his eyes, Adam asked, "Would you like me to say a prayer for you today?"

"Yes, that would be a blessing for me. Thank you...and thank you for letting me borrow your car."

Zinc went down the stairs to the market, then out to the loading dock where the Walker's Buick was parked. He packed the groceries into the back seat and started the car. Before putting it into gear, he prayed, "Please be with me dear God. Help me to do and say the right things today."

It took only a few minutes to finish the drive to Lady Remington's mansion home, *Mom Remington's home*. Zinc pulled up to the circular drive and waited in the car a few minutes. He didn't see any movement inside her home. For a fraction of a second, he thought he would just put the car in reverse and go back to the market—back to where it was safe. But what was unsafe here, the unknown?

Three years ago, if he was afraid of the unknown, he would not be the Zinc he was now. But oh gosh, he was overthinking what was before him in that house. Instead, Zinc said another quick prayer for guidance and opened the car door. From the back seat, he took the brown paper bags of groceries in his in arms and walked up onto the front porch. The heavy wooden front door was wide-open, showing only the screen door.

Holding both bags, Zinc called from the front porch into the house.

"Lady Remington, can I come in? I have your groceries from the market."

From somewhere inside, Lady Remington answered, "Are you the regular delivery boy? Your voice doesn't sound like him. Just place the groceries on the porch bench, and I will get them later."

"Okay, I can do that, but could I talk with you a little? Please?"

Zinc could hear the sound of high heels clicking on the wide-planked flooring as she came to the door and opened it. For a long moment, she looked into Zinc's eyes, then dropped her gaze away.

"I don't have much company, you know, but you look like a nice man. I guess I can sit a spell or two with you."

Just before opening the screen door, Lady Remington straightened her black dress, then guided a few strands of her black hair away from her face with the tip of her fingers. Zinc watched her slight form as she went to sit down on the porch bench. He had inherited her wide shoulders and her generous height. For an older woman, she still possessed grace and even some charm, although hidden by emotional pain. Zinc carefully sat down next to her on the same bench.

"Lady Remington, would you allow me to call you another name…that is if you don't mind?"

"Well, my first name is Geranium, so you can call me that. I always loved that name."

"Thank you… Geranium. Yes, that is a really pretty name."

Without exchanging words, they both sat looking straight ahead enjoying the seagrass, which was planted on a slight mound in the center of her lawn. The grass danced back and forth from the soft breeze, blowing in from the ocean. Now that September was fast approaching, the tassels were well-developed and were starting to become a golden straw color. These were the same variety that Geranium planted on the sandy bank to keep erosion from taking away Gray Cliff lighthouse. But that was years ago, and now she was sitting with a young man whom she just met—both sharing the afternoon together.

"Geranium, I don't know how to say this any other way, so here it goes. The man Marvin Bitter died in City General Hospital a week ago. I know this because I happened to be there with Pastor Westman. I saw Marvin die right before my eyes."

Zinc was now looking directly at Geranium. He saw the stressed wrinkles fade a little from her face. Her breathing now was like someone who had a terrible burden lifted from her shoulders; it was full and peaceful. She then also turned toward Zinc. Looking into his eyes, she allowed the words from his lips to carry healing, which traveled deep into her very soul.

Zinc knew he had to measure how he would share his next revelation.

"Geranium, can we continue sitting here together on your bench a little longer? I have something more to tell you."

He allowed the silence between them to bath their emotions with more healing. Geranium thought for a while, thinking of all the years she withdrew from making any close friendships. Now within these few moments, she felt so close to this young man sitting next to her. She thought about that as she used the heels on her shoes as a pivot to rock her feet up and down slightly, matching the easy rhythm of her breathing.

In a surprising way, she did not want this time together with Zinc to end. But he had more to say to her, so she nodded her head in a *yes* fashion a few times. Zinc started to form his words, but then with her loving touch, Geranium tenderly placed her hand on his and said:

"Zinc… Zinc…you are…my son. Right?"

Zinc said, "Yes… *Mom*…yes, I am your son."

Both mom and son were now holding each other, sharing some soft crying together. During this time, it seemed that no one else in the world existed. After so many years, it was the reunion that finally happened.

Zinc's mom then gathered her words, those she never thought would ever happen until they met in heaven. Just before she started her story, Zinc thought of Sherriff Jake's walk with him. He would now hear the words directly from his mom.

"I am sorry to say this, but Marvin was a horrible man. Years before you were born, he had alcohol demons, and it led him to do terrible things. He would be gone from the house for months at a time drinking and carousing with all kinds of trampy women. When he finally came back home, it was to physically beat me then go to work at the docks.

"I'm not proud of this, but during the last time he was gone, I fell in love with a wonderful man. Yes, I had an affair, but you were conceived in love from that. *Zinc, you were conceived in love.* Marvin continued to drink not even knowing I was pregnant…for your protection and mine, I kept that from him. After giving birth to you and coming back from the hospital with you in my arms, he committed me to a mental hospital. Eight months later, when I was released, he met me at the hospital gate and told me never to contact you or him or any of our friends, else he would kill me. He even changed your name! The name I originally gave you was my dear father's name *Christopher*, meaning carrier of Christ."

"Zinc, my son, until now, I had no idea you were my Christopher. I have kept to myself, staying away from everyone all these years for my own protection… I was so afraid. I also hated that man so much so that I started to use my maiden name. I couldn't possibly carry *his* name around with me."

Zinc had only love for this woman, and he continued to hold her hands. From his fingers, he could feel both of their pulses that seemed to beat at the very same time. They shared time and tender conversation for several more hours that afternoon. Zinc did not want to leave her; she needed his love and attention. However, he did not know then how she would need his tender care, especially toward evenings. She would continue to fantasize while playing the piano in her living room.

After they were both exhausted from emotions, Zinc looked at her hands again and then at her peaceful face and asked:

"Next year, when I get out of the Army, can
I come here to live with you?"

"Yes, Zinc…my son…this is just not a house, *this is your home.*"

EPILOGUE

People of God

Zinc

Thank you, sir or madam, for reading about a portion of my life. It was a privilege that I could share this time with you. So the remaining year in the Army went fast since in the service, there was an endless need for my welding skills. As a matter of fact, in my fourth year, I was asked if I wanted to conduct welding training classes for new Army recruits. Well, I jumped at the opportunity, which also gave me an Army promotion to Corporal E-4. At the end of my enlistment, our sergeant tried to convince me to stay in the service and make it an Army career. However, after talking with me, he admitted I would have a trade in the civilian market that would work quite nicely.

The sergeant was right as usual. I found work in a steel fabrication company, which pays well, and I liked it there. In six months, I was promoted to supervisor, where I oversaw the construction of steel trusses for City General Hospital's endless expansions. One of those expansions included a unit for the treatment and recovery of children with cancer.

While at my home, I enjoyed every evening together with my mom. If Geranium started to fantasize, then I lovingly became her audience. Believe me, I never experienced such compassion in her music, and every night she played, I was completely spellbound.

It was five years later, during the middle of winter, that God called Geranium home to play for the angels in heaven. I remembered it so well. I arrived a little late from work to see my loving mom sitting on her piano bench using her arms crisscrossed over the keyboard for a pillow. The following week after her funeral, I legally changed my name to Christopher, *Christopher Remington*.

Are you ready for this? Two years later, I met a really pretty Christian girl at a religious retreat. At the age of twenty-nine, I asked Pastor Westman to perform our wedding ceremony for me and my lovely bride-to-be. It was a privilege to have Walt for my best man, and of course, our beautiful wedding reception was at the Tinker's barn. As you might guess, it was extremely elegant, and Carmen and George did such a wonderful job for us and our guests.

May I add one more thing that I feel is important? Thank you. When I visited my dad in that hospital room, on his last day here on earth, I was not prepared for how I would react. God gave me one more gift that day. Yes, I did forgive my dad for all his twisted treatment he gave me. In that moment, I truly forgave him. Truly forgiving him is what released me of a burden inside my soul. I found that I could love again, only by first forgiving, and forgiving completely. See, that forgiveness was *a blessing to my dad, but even more for me*. Thank you, almighty and perfect God!

George and Carmen

Hello friends! After Nichole and Patrick's wedding, my lovely wife and I expanded our restaurant business to include delightful dinners hosted in the barn. We named our barn, *Fienile Eleganza*, which we believe is Italian for elegant barn, and everyone says it truly is elegant. Our sold-out event include celebrations for Mother's Day, maple syrup production, cherry picking, Father's Day, summer solstice, blueberry gathering and several apple festivals, one for each variety. If a young couple is fortunate enough, we are able to host their wedding reception at Fienile Eleganza. I am not bragging since we believe it was not at all our plan, but *God's*…but any reservations have to be made well in advance. There is always a waiting list. We still are able to give 10% of our earnings to our church, another blessing.

Carmen made a little sketch of our Fienile Eleganza for our marketing flyers. You can see it below. God bless you, your family and your friends. One more thing. I don't mean to sound "preachy" but please always thank God for your blessings. *He always wants to hear from all of us.*

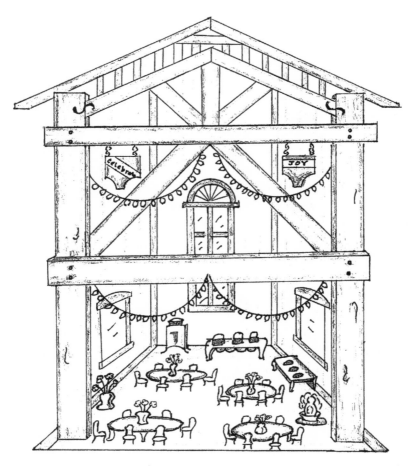

FIENILE ELEGANZA

Adam and Silvia

We worked another ten years, then we gave the business to our energetic son, Walt. Walt had kept busy at the market, but not so much that he didn't have time to date. My wife, Silvia, told Walt to find a nice girl from our church to marry. A few years ago—yes, in church—he found his true love, a black-haired, blue-eyed beauty. In their first few years of marriage, they worked together and renovated a Port James Victorian home. When that project was completed, they used the third bedroom as a nursery for their firstborn.

Walt kept the mechanical horse in the market, which is still a working attraction for children. The coffee bean grinder is used daily, but the tube tester is not used anymore. It still stands in the back of the market as a reminder of days gone by.

So we have already—and God willing—still be able to enjoy many outings together. We love to explore historical coastal towns, staying in quaint bed and breakfasts along the way. While I drive, Silvia always looks for lighthouses. For those that are open to the public, we climb the winding staircases to the top and share breathtaking ocean views with each other. She still wears the silver neckless I gave her a while ago at the top of Gray Cliff lighthouse. Gosh, by now, that must have been fifteen years or more ago. Yes, that was my incurable romantic side, right? In many ways, we feel like newlyweds, having fun. In a few months, we are both looking forward to spoiling our first grandchild with presents on his upcoming second birthday.

We believe life is good in Port James. We absolutely believe God gives us His daily love. Thank you, God, for being you.

Sherriff Jake

I took some time to decide this, and so at the age of sixty-one, I am now retired from the police force. My pension is not huge but is enough for us to enjoy our lifestyle here in Port James. I am having fun in my postage stamp-sized backyard, grilling in the evenings with my family. While continuing walks in the village, my grandchildren are more than happy to walk with me. To their delight, stops are made at Beth's Bakery.

Yes, I know, without having to be in such great shape for my job, I have gained a little weight around my middle area. So be it. I enjoy sharing a blueberry turnover or two as the grandkids dive into theirs. In between munching, I find endless stories to share and delight with each wide-eyed little munchkins.

May I add one more thing please? Thank you. One morning, a few days ago, I was walking my tour in town and saw my friend Adam looking up into the heavens. He did not see me, but I heard him whisper something while looking at the blue sky and white clouds. He simply said, "Good morning, God." It stopped me in my tracks as I thought about this for a moment. What a nice way to start your day, don't you think so? "Good morning God."

Friends, would you be willing to greet our God every morning in this special way? Can you imagine each and every day thousands of believers, *including you*, going outside, looking up into the sky and saying, "Good morning, God!" Imagine you and so many souls all across the world, living in villages, towns, cities, and rural country-side all making this special connection to our Maker. I also believe that our Creator would totally and absolutely love this!

For everything that is good, thank you, God. In good times as well as in times of trial, thank you for always being with us.

You are the true and perfect love for all creation!

IF YOU LIKED THIS BOOK, YOU'LL ALSO LIKE...

Klem Watercrest, The Lighthouse Keeper
by Jay Diedreck

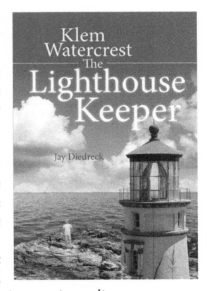

Much of Port James has been untouched somehow from many of the hassles of our times. Klem Watercrest, the delightful lighthouse keeper and main character, brings insight to friends and family, many times while tending to the community lighthouse.

Be prepared to enjoy a delightful, religious, yet an adventuresome story of a Maine seaside village and its precious and unforgettable residents.

It is a book that you may not want to put down. Readers have said that it is captivating right through to its surprise ending.

ABOUT THE AUTHOR

A resident of the village of Spencerport New York for six decades, Jay and his beloved wife, Alicia, still treasure every day as a gift from God. They enjoy sharing their grandchildren's activities such as storytelling, sport competitions, and concerts. They also find time for their own outings of exploring quaint towns and  canoeing along the Erie Canal and the beautiful streams of western New York.